"I'm Not Going Away With You."

"This isn't going to die down." He kept his voice even and low, reasonable. The stakes were too important for all of them. "The reporters will swarm you by morning, if not sooner. Your friends will sell photos of the two of us together."

"Then we're through, you and I."

"Do you honestly think anyone's going to believe the breakup is for real? The timing will seem too convenient."

"We ended things last weekend."

Like hell. "Tell that to the papers and see if they believe you. Pleading a breakup isn't going to buy you any kind of freedom from their interest."

She studied him through narrowed eyes. "How do I know you're not just using this as an excuse to get back together?"

Was he? An hour ago, he would have done anything to get into her bed again.

Dear Reader,

Welcome to my world of the Rich, Rugged & Royal
Medina family! I've always been a fan of fairy tales
about princes and princesses earning their happily
ever after. In deciding to create my own fairy tale
royal family, I was entranced by the possibility that
a prince could be living incognito right next door.
From that emerged the deposed royal patriarch King
Enrique Medina (who in my mind looks just like
Sean Connery) and his three sons.

In *The Maverick Prince,* you'll meet the youngest
Medina heir, Antonio, at just the moment his identity
is exposed, much to the surprise of his new lover.
I hope you enjoy Antonio and Shannon's passionate
journey from Texas to Florida in search of true love.
Stay tuned for Duarte Medina's story in January and
Carlos Medina's book in March.

Happy reading!

Catherine Mann

www.catherinemann.com

CATHERINE MANN

THE MAVERICK PRINCE

Published by Silhouette Books
America's Publisher of Contemporary Romance

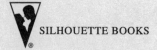 SILHOUETTE BOOKS

Recycling programs
for this product may
not exist in your area.

ISBN-13: 978-0-373-73060-5

THE MAVERICK PRINCE

Copyright © 2010 by Catherine Mann

Visit Silhouette Books at www.eHarlequin.com

Printed in U.S.A.

Books by Catherine Mann

Silhouette Desire

Baby, I'm Yours #1721
Under the Millionaire's Influence #1787
The Executive's Surprise Baby #1837
†*Rich Man's Fake Fiancée* #1878
†*His Expectant Ex* #1895
Propositioned Into a Foreign Affair #1941
†*Millionaire in Command* #1969
Bossman's Baby Scandal #1988
†*The Tycoon Takes a Wife* #2013
Winning It All #2031
   "Pregnant with the Playboy's Baby"
*The Maverick Prince #2047

*Rich, Rugged & Royal
†The Landis Brothers

CATHERINE MANN

USA TODAY bestselling author Catherine Mann is living out her own fairy-tale ending on a sunny Florida beach with her prince-charming husband and their four children. With more than thirty-five books in print in over twenty countries, she has also celebrated wins for both a RITA® Award and a Booksellers' Best Award. Catherine enjoys chatting with readers online—thanks to the wonders of the wireless internet that allows her to network with her laptop by the water! To learn more about her work, visit her website, www.catherinemann.com, or reach her by snail mail at P.O. Box 6065, Navarre, FL 32566.

To my favorite little princesses and princes—
Megan, Frances, James and Zach. Thank you for inviting
Aunt Cathy to your prince and princess tea parties.
The snack cakes and Sprite were absolutely magical!

Prologue

Royalty Revealed!

Do you have a prince living next door? Quite possibly!

Courtesy of a positive identification made by one of the GlobalIntruder.com's very own photojournalists, we've successfully landed the scoop of the year. The deposed Medina monarchy has not, as was rumored, set up shop in a highly secured fortress in Argentina. The three Medina heirs—with their billions—have been living under assumed names and rubbing elbows with everyday Americans for decades.

We hear the sexy baby of the family, Antonio, is already taken in Texas by his waitress girlfriend

Shannon Crawford. She'd better watch her back now that word is out about her secret shipping magnate!

Meanwhile, never fear, ladies. There are still two single and studly Medina men left. Our sources reveal that Duarte dwells in his plush resort in Martha's Vineyard. Carlos—a surgeon, no less—resides in Tacoma. Wonder if he makes house calls?

No word yet on their father, King Enrique Medina, former ruler of San Rinaldo, an island off the coast of Spain. But our best reporters are hot on the trail.

For the latest update on how to nab a prince, check back in with the GlobalIntruder.com. And remember, you heard it here first!

One

"King takes the queen." Antonio Medina declared his victory and raked in the chips, having bluffed with a simple high-card hand in Texas Hold'Em.

Ignoring an incoming call on his iPhone, he stacked his winnings. He didn't often have time for poker since his fishing charter company went global, but joining backroom games at his pal Vernon's Galveston Bay Grille had become a more frequent occurrence of late. Since Shannon. His gaze snapped to the long skinny windows on either side of the door leading out to the main dining area where she worked.

No sign of Shannon's slim body, winding her way through the brass, crystal and white linen of the five-star restaurant. Disappointment chewed at him in spite of his win.

A cell phone chime cut the air, then a second right

afterward. Not his either time, although the noise still forced his focus back to the private table while two of Vernon Wolfe's cronies pressed the ignore button, cutting the ringing short. Vernon's poker pals were all about forty years senior to Antonio. But the old shrimp-boat captain turned restaurateur had saved Antonio's bacon back when he'd been a teen. So if Vernon beckoned, Antonio did his damnedest to show. The fact that Shannon also worked here provided extra oomph to the request.

Vernon creaked back in the leather chair, also disregarding his cell phone currently crooning "Son of a Sailor" from his belt. "Ballsy move holding with just a king, Tony," he said, his voice perpetually raspy from years of shouting on deck. His face still sported a year-round tan, eyes raccoon ringed from sunglasses. "I thought Glenn had a royal flush with his queen and jack showing."

"I was taught to bluff by the best." Antonio—or Tony Castillo as he was known these days—grinned.

A smile was more disarming than a scowl. He always smiled so nobody knew what he was thinking. Not that even his best grin had gained him forgiveness from Shannon after their fight last weekend.

Resisting the urge to frown, Tony stacked his chips on the scarred wooden table Vernon had pried from his boat before docking himself permanently at the restaurant. "Your pal Glenn needs to bluff better."

Glenn—a coffee addict—chugged his java faster when bluffing. For some reason no one else seemed to notice as the high-priced attorney banged back his third brew laced with Irish whiskey. He then simply shrugged, loosened his silk tie and hooked it on the back of the chair, settling in for the next round.

Vernon swept up the played cards, flipping the king of hearts between his fingers until the cell stopped singing vintage Jimmy Buffett. "Keep winning and they're not going to let me deal you in anymore."

Tony went through the motions of laughing along, but he knew he wasn't going anywhere. This was his world now. He'd built a life of his own and wanted nothing to do with the Medina name. He was Tony Castillo now. His father had honored that. Until recently.

For the past six months, his deposed king of a dad had sent message after message demanding his presence at the secluded island compound off the coast of Florida. Tony had left that gilded prison the second he'd turned eighteen and never looked back. If Enrique was as sick as he claimed, then their problems would have to be sorted out in heaven...or more likely in somewhere hotter even than Texas.

While October meant autumn chills for folks like his two brothers, he preferred the lengthened summers in Galveston Bay. The air conditioner still cranked in the redbrick waterside restaurant in the historic district.

Muffled live music from a flamenco guitarist drifted through the wall along with the drone of dining clientele. Business was booming for Vernon. Tony made sure of that. Vernon had given Antonio a job at eighteen when no one else would trust a kid with sketchy ID. Fourteen years and many millions of dollars later, Tony figured it was only fair some of the proceeds from the shipping business he'd built should buy the aging shrimp-boat captain a retirement plan.

Vernon nudged the deck toward Glenn to cut, then dealt the next hand. Glenn shoved his buzzing BlackBerry beside his spiked coffee and thumbed his cards up for a peek.

Tony reached for his...and stopped...tipping his ear toward the sound from outside the door. A light laugh cut through the clanging dishes and fluttering strum of the

Spanish guitar. *Her* laugh. Finally. The simple sound made him ache after a week without her.

His gaze shot straight to the door again, bracketed by two windows showcasing the dining area. Shannon stepped in view of the left lengthy pane, pausing to punch in an order at the servers' station. She squinted behind her cat-eye glasses, the retros giving her a naughty schoolmarm look that never failed to send his libido surging.

Light from the globed sconces glinted on her pale blond hair. She wore her long locks in a messy updo, as much a part of her work uniform as the knee-length black skirt and form-fitting tuxedo vest. She looked sexy as hell—and exhausted.

Damn it all, he would help her without hesitation. Just last weekend he'd suggested as much when she'd pulled on her clothes after they'd made love at his Bay Shore mansion. She'd shut him down faster than the next heartbeat. In fact, she hadn't spoken to him or returned his calls since.

Stubborn, sexy woman. It wasn't like he'd offered to set her up as his mistress, for crying out loud. He was only trying to help her and her three-year-old son. She always vowed she would do anything for Kolby.

Mentioning that part hadn't gone well for him, either.

Her lips had pursed tight, but her eyes behind those sexy black glasses had told him she wanted to throw his offer back in his face. His ears still rang from the slamming door when she'd walked out. Most women he knew would have jumped at the prospect of money or expensive gifts. Not Shannon. If anything, she seemed put off by his wealth. It had taken him two months to persuade her just to have coffee with him. Then two more months to work his way into bed with her. And after nearly four weeks of mind-bending sex, he was still no closer to understanding her.

Okay, so he'd built a fortune from Galveston Bay being

one of the largest importers of seafood. Luck had played a part by landing him here in the first place. He'd simply been looking for a coastal community that reminded him of home.

His real home, off the coast of Spain. Not the island fortress his father had built off the U.S. The one he'd escaped the day he'd turned eighteen and swapped his last name from Medina to Castillo. The new surname had been plucked from one of the many branches twigging off his regal family tree. Tony *Castillo* had vowed never to return, a vow he'd kept.

And he didn't even want to think about how spooked Shannon would be if she knew the well-kept secret of his royal heritage. Not that the secret was his to share.

Vernon tapped the scarred wooden table in front of him. "Your phone's buzzing again. We can hold off on this hand while you take the call."

Tony thumbed the ignore button on his iPhone without looking. He only disregarded the outside world for two people, Shannon and Vernon. "It's about the Salinas Shrimp deal. They need to sweat for another hour before we settle on the bottom line."

Glenn rolled his coffee mug between his palms. "So when we don't hear back from you, we'll all know you hit the ignore button."

"Never," Tony responded absently, tucking the device back inside his suit coat. More and more he looked forward to Shannon's steady calm at the end of a hectic day.

Vernon's phone chimed again—Good God, what was up with all the interruptions?—this time rumbling with Marvin Gaye's "Let's Get It On."

The grizzled captain slapped down his cards. "That's my wife. Gotta take this one." Bluetooth glowing in his ear, he shot to his feet and tucked into a corner for semiprivacy. "Yeah, sugar?"

Since Vernon had just tied the knot for the first time seven months ago, the guy acted like a twenty-year-old newlywed. Tony walled off flickering thoughts of his own parents' marriage, not too hard since there weren't that many to remember. His mother had died when he was five.

Vernon inhaled sharply. Tony looked up. His old mentor's face paled under a tan so deep it almost seemed tattooed. What the hell?

"Tony." Vernon's voice went beyond raspy, like the guy had swallowed ground glass. "I think you'd better check those missed messages."

"Is something wrong?" he asked, already reaching for his iPhone.

"You'll have to tell us that," Vernon answered without once taking his raccoonlike eyes off Tony. "Actually, you can skip the messages and just head straight for the internet."

"Where?" He tapped through the menu.

"Anywhere." Vernon sank back into his chair like an anchor thudding to the bottom of the ocean floor. "It's headlining everywhere. You won't miss it."

His iPhone connected to the internet and displayed the top stories—

Royalty Revealed!
Medina Monarchy Exposed!

Blinking fast, he stared in shock at the last thing he expected, but the outcome his father had always feared most. One heading at a time, his family's cover was peeled away until he settled on the last in the list.

Meet the Medina Mistress!

The insane speed of viral news… His gaze shot straight to the windows separating him from the waiters' station, where seconds ago he'd seen Shannon.

Sure enough, she still stood with her back to him. He wouldn't have much time. He had to talk to her before she finished tapping in her order or tabulating a bill.

Tony shot to his feet, his chair scraping loudly in the silence as Vernon's friends all checked their messages. Reaching for the brass handle, he kept his eyes locked on the woman who turned him inside out with one touch of her hand on his bare flesh, the simple brush of her hair across his chest until he forgot about staying on guard. Foreboding crept up his spine. His instincts had served him well over the years—steering him through multimillion-dollar business decisions, even warning him of a frayed shrimp net inching closer to snag his feet.

And before all that? The extra sense had powered his stride as he'd raced through the woods, running from rebels overthrowing San Rinaldo's government. Rebels who hadn't thought twice about shooting at kids, even a five-year-old.

Or murdering their mother.

The Medina cover was about more than privacy. It was about safety. While his family had relocated to a U.S. island after the coup, they could never let down their guard. And damn it all, he'd selfishly put Shannon in the crosshairs simply because he had to have her in his bed.

Tony clasped her shoulders and turned her around. Only to stop short.

Her beautiful blue eyes wide with horror said it all. And if he'd been in doubt? The cell phone clutched in Shannon's hand told him the rest.

She already knew.

* * *

She didn't want to know.

The internet rumor her son's babysitter had read over the phone had to be a media mistake. As did the five follow-up articles she'd found in her own ten-second search with her cell's internet service.

The blogosphere could bloom toxic fiction in minutes, right? People could say whatever they wanted, make a fortune off click-throughs and then retract the erroneous story the next day. Tony's touch on her shoulders was so familiar and stirring he simply couldn't be a stranger. Even now her body warmed at the feel of his hands until she swayed.

But then hadn't she made the very same mistake with her dead husband, buying into his facade because she *wanted* it to be true?

Damn it, Tony wasn't Nolan. All of this would be explained away and she could go back to her toe-curling affair with Tony. Except they were already in the middle of a fight over trying to give her money—an offer that made her skin crawl. And if he was actually a prince?

She swallowed hysterical laughter. Well, he'd told her that he had money to burn and it could very well be he'd meant that on a scale far grander than she could have ever imagined.

"Breathe," her ex-lover commanded.

"Okay, okay, okay," she chanted on each gasp of air, tapping her glasses more firmly in place in hopes the dots in front of her eyes would fade. "I'm okay."

Now that her vision cleared she had a better view of her place at the center of the restaurant's attention. And when had Tony started edging her toward the door? Impending doom welled inside her as she realized the local media would soon descend.

"Good, steady now, in and out." His voice didn't sound any different.

But it also didn't sound Texan. Or southern. Or even northern for that matter, as if he'd worked to stamp out any sense of regionality from himself. She tried to focus on the timbre that so thoroughly strummed her senses when they made love.

"Tony, please say we're going to laugh over this misunderstanding later."

He didn't answer. His square jaw was set and serious as he looked over her shoulder, scanning. She found no signs of her carefree lover, even though her fingers carried the memory of how his dark hair curled around her fingers. His wealth and power had been undeniable from the start in his clothes and lifestyle, but most of all in his proud carriage. Now she took new note of his aristocratic jaw and cheekbones. Such a damn handsome and charming man. She'd allowed herself to be wowed. Seduced by his smile.

She'd barely come to grips with dating a rich guy, given all the bad baggage that brought up of her dead husband. A crooked sleaze. She'd been dazzled by Nolan's glitzy world, learning too late it was financed by a Ponzi scheme.

The guilt of those destroyed lives squeezed the breath from her lungs all over again. If not for her son, she might very well have curled inside herself and given up after Nolan took his own life. But she would hold strong for Kolby.

"Answer me," she demanded, hoping.

"This isn't the place to talk."

Not reassuring and, oh God, why did Tony still have the power to hurt her? Anger punched through the pain. "How long does it take to say *damned rumor?*"

He slid an arm around her shoulders, tucking her to his side. "Let's find somewhere more private."

"Tell me now." She pulled back from the lure of his familiar scent, minty patchouli and sandalwood, the smell of exotic pleasures.

Tony—Antonio—Prince Medina—whoever the hell he was—ducked his head closer to hers. "Shannon, do you really want to talk here where anyone can listen? The world's going to intrude on our town soon enough."

Tears burned behind her eyes, the room going blurry even with her glasses on. "Okay, we'll find a quiet place to discuss this."

He backed her toward the kitchen. Her legs and his synched up in step, her hips following his instinctively, as if they'd danced together often…and more. Eyes and whispers followed them the entire way. Did everyone already know? Cell phones sang from pockets and vibrated on tabletops as if Galveston quivered on the verge of an earthquake.

No one approached them outright, but fragments drifted from their huddled discussions.

"Could Tony Castillo be—"

"—Medina—"

"—With that waitress—"

The buzz increased like a swarm of locusts closing in on the Texas landscape. On her life.

Tony growled lowly, "There's nowhere here we can speak privately. I need to get you out of Vernon's."

His muscled arm locked her tighter, guiding her through a swishing door, past a string of chefs all immobile and gawking. He shouldered out a side door and she had no choice but to follow.

Outside, the late-day sun kissed his bronzed face, bringing his deeply tanned features into sharper focus. She'd always known there was something strikingly foreign about him. But she'd believed his story of dead parents, bookkeepers who'd emigrated from South America. Her own parents had died in a car accident before she'd graduated from college. She'd thought they'd at least shared similar childhoods.

Now? She was sure of nothing except how her body still betrayed her with the urge to lean into his hard-muscled strength, to escape into the pleasure she knew he could bring.

"I need to let management know I'm leaving. I can't lose this job." Tips were best in the evening and she needed every penny. She couldn't afford the time it would take to get her teaching credentials current again—if she could even find a music-teaching position with cutbacks in the arts.

And there weren't too many people out there in search of private oboe lessons.

"I know the owner, remember?" He unlocked his car, the remote chirp-chirping.

"Of course. What was I thinking? You have connections." She stifled a fresh bout of hysterical laughter.

Would she even be able to work again if the Medina rumor was true? It had been tough enough finding a job when others associated her with her dead husband. Sure, she'd been cleared of any wrongdoing, but many still believed she must have known about Nolan's illegal schemes.

There hadn't even been a trial for her to state her side. Once her husband had made bail, he'd been dead within twenty-four hours.

Tony cursed low and harsh, sailor-style swearing he usually curbed around her and Kolby. She looked around, saw nothing… Then she heard the thundering footsteps a second before the small cluster of people rounded the corner with cameras and microphones.

Swearing again, Tony yanked open the passenger door to his Escalade. He lifted her inside easily, as if she weighed nothing more than the tray of fried gator appetizers she'd carried earlier.

Seconds later he slid behind the wheel and slammed the door a hair's breadth ahead of the reporters. Fists pounded on the tinted windows. Locks auto-clicked. Shannon sagged in the leather seat with relief.

The hefty SUV rocked from the force of the mob. Her heart rate ramped again. If this was the life of the rich and famous, she wanted no part.

Shifting into Reverse then forward, Tony drove, slow but steady. People peeled away. At least one reporter fell on his butt but everyone appeared unharmed.

So much for playing chicken with Tony. She would be wise to remember that.

He guided the Escalade through the historic district a hint over the speed limit, fast enough to put space between them and the media hounds. Panting in the aftermath, she still braced a hand on the dash, her other gripping the leather seat. Yet Tony hadn't even broken a sweat.

His hands stayed steady on the wheel, his expensive watch glinting from the French cuffs of his shirt. Restored brick buildings zipped by her window. A young couple dressed for an evening out stepped off the curb, then back sharply. While the whole idea of being hunted by the paparazzi scared her to her roots, right here in the SUV with Tony, she felt safe.

Safe enough for the anger and betrayal to come bubbling to the surface. She'd been mad at him since their fight last weekend over his continued insistence on giving her money.

But those feelings were nothing compared to the rage that coursed through her now. "We're alone. Talk to me."

"It's complicated." He glanced in the rearview mirror. Normal traffic tooled along the narrow street. "What do you want to know?"

She forced herself to say the words that would drive a permanent wedge between her and the one man she'd dared let into her life again.

"Are you a part of that lost royal family, the one everybody thought was hiding in Argentina?"

The Cadillac's finely tuned engine hummed in the silence. Lights clicked on automatically with the setting sun, the dash glowing.

His knuckles went white on the steering wheel, his jaw flexing before he nodded tightly. "The rumors on the internet are correct."

And she'd thought her heart couldn't break again.

Her pride had been stung over Tony's offer to give her money, but she would have gotten over it. She would have stuck to her guns about paying her own way, of course. But *this?* It was still too huge to wrap her brain around. She'd slept with a prince, let him into her home, her body, and considered letting him into her heart. His deception burned deep.

How could she have missed the truth so completely, buying into his stories about working on a shrimp boat as a teen? She'd assumed his tattoo and the closed over pierced earlobe were parts of an everyman past that seduced her as fully as his caresses.

"Your name isn't even Tony Castillo." Oh God. She pressed the back of her hand against her mouth, suddenly nauseated because she didn't even know the name of the guy she'd been sleeping with.

"Technically, it could be."

Shannon slammed her fists against the leather seat instead of reaching for him as she ached to do. "I'm not interested in technically. Actually, I'm not interested in people who lie to me. Can I even trust that you're really thirty-two years old?"

"It isn't just my decision to share specific details. I have other family members to consider. But if it's any consolation, I really am thirty-two. Are you really twenty-nine?"

"I'm not in a joking mood." Shivering, she thumbed her bare ring finger where once a three-carat diamond had rested. After Nolan's funeral, she'd taken it off and sold it along with everything else to pay off the mountain of debt. "I should have known you were too good to be true."

"Why do you say that?"

"Who makes millions by thirty-two?"

He cocked an arrogant eyebrow. "Did you just call me a moocher?"

"Well, excuse me if that was rude, but I'm not exactly at my best tonight."

His arms bulged beneath his Italian suit—she'd had to look up the exclusive Garaceni label after she'd seen the coat hanging on his bedpost.

Tony looked even more amazing out of the clothes, his tanned and muscled body eclipsing any high-end wardrobe. And the smiles he brought to her life, his uninhibited laughter were just what she needed most.

How quiet her world had been without him this week. "Sorry to have hurt your feelings, pal. Or should I say, Your Majesty? Since according to some of those stories I'm 'His Majesty's mistress.'"

"Actually, it would be 'Your Highness.'" His signature smile tipped his mouth, but with a bitter edge. "Majesty is for the king."

How could he be so flippant? "Actually, you can take your title and stuff it where the sun—"

"I get the picture." He guided the Escalade over the Galveston Island Causeway, waves moving darkly below. "You'll need time to calm down so we can discuss how to handle this."

"You don't understand. There's no calming down. You lied to me on a fundamental level. Once we made l—" she stumbled over the next word, images of him moving over her, inside her, stealing her words and breath until her stomach churned as fast as the waters below "—after we went to bed together, you should have told me. Unless the sex didn't mean anything special to you. I guess if you had to tell every woman you slept with, there would be no secret."

"Stop!" He sliced the air with his hand. His gleaming Patek Philippe watch contrasted with scarred knuckles, from his sailing days he'd once told her. "That's not true and not the point here. You were safer not knowing."

"Oh, it's for my own good." She wrapped her arms around herself, a shield from the hurt.

"How much do you know about my family's history?"

She bit back the urge to snap at him. Curiosity reined in her temper. "Not much. Just that there was a king of some small country near Spain, I think, before he was overthrown in a coup. His family has been hiding out to avoid the paparazzi hoopla."

"Hoopla? This might suck, but that's the least of my worries. There are people out there who tried to kill my family and succeeded in murdering my mother. There are people who stand to gain a lot in the way of money and power if the Medinas are wiped off the planet."

Her heart ached for all he had lost. Even now, she wanted to press her mouth to his and forget this whole insane mess.

To grasp that shimmering connection she'd discovered with him the first time they'd made love in a frenzied tangle at his Galveston Bay mansion.

"Well, believe it, Shannon. There's a big bad world outside your corner of Texas. Right now, some of the worst will start focusing on me, my family and anyone who's close to us. Whether you like it or not, I'll do whatever it takes to keep you and Kolby protected."

Her son's safety? Perspiration froze on her forehead, chilling her deeper. Why hadn't she thought of that? Of course she'd barely wrapped her brain around Tony... Antonio. "Drive faster. Get me home now."

"I completely agree. I've already sent bodyguards ahead of us."

Bodyguards?

"When?" She'd barely been able to think, much less act. What kind of mother was she not to have considered the impact on Kolby? And what kind of man kept bodyguards on speed dial?

"I texted my people while we were leaving through the kitchen."

Of course he had people. The man was not merely the billionaire shipping magnate she'd assumed, he was also the bearer of a surname generations old and a background of privilege she couldn't begin to fathom.

"I was so distracted I didn't even notice," Shannon whispered, sinking into her seat. She wasn't even safe in her own neighborhood anymore.

She couldn't wish this away any longer. "You really are this Medina guy. You're really from some deposed royal family."

His chin tipped with unmistakable regality. "My name is Antonio Medina. I was born in San Rinaldo, third son of King Enrique and Queen Beatriz."

Her heart drumming in her ears, panic squeezed harder at her rib cage. How could she have foreseen this when she met him five months ago at the restaurant, bringing his supper back to the owner's poker game? Tony had ordered a shrimp po'boy sandwich and a glass of sweet tea.

Poor Boy? How ironic was that?

"This is too weird." And scary.

The whole surreal mess left her too numb to hurt anymore. That would return later, for sure. Her hands shook as she tapped her glasses straight.

She had to stay focused now. "Stuff like this happens in movies or a hundred years ago."

"Or in my life. Now in yours, too."

"Nuh-uh. You and I?" She waggled her hand back and forth between them. "We're history."

He paused at a stop sign, turning to face her fully for the first time since he'd gripped her shoulders at the restaurant. His coal black eyes heated over her, a bold man of uninhibited emotions. "That fast, you're ready to call an end to what we've shared?"

Her heart picked up speed from just the caress of his eyes, the memory of his hands stroking her. She tried to answer but her mouth had gone dry. He skimmed those scarred knuckles down her arm until his hand rested on hers. Such a simple gesture, nothing overtly erotic, but her whole body hummed with awareness and want.

Right here in the middle of the street, in the middle of an upside down situation, her body betrayed her as surely as he had.

Wrong. Wrong. Wrong. She had to be tough. "I already ended things between us last weekend."

"That was a fight, not a breakup." His big hand splayed over hers, eclipsing her with heat.

"Semantics. Not that it matters." She pulled herself

away from him until her spine met the door, not nearly far enough. "I can't be with you anymore."

"That's too damn bad, because we're going to be spending a lot of time together after we pick up your son. There's no way you can stay in your apartment tonight."

"There's no way I can stay with *you*."

"You can't hide from what's been unleashed. Today should tell you that more than anything. It'll find you and your son. I'm sorry for not seeing this coming, but it's here and we have to deal with it."

Fear for her son warred with her anger at Tony. "You had no right," she hissed between clenched teeth, "no right at all to play with our lives this way."

"I agree." He surprised her with that. However, the reprieve was short. "But I'm the only one who can stand between you both and whatever fallout comes from this revelation."

Two

A bodyguard stood outside the front door of her first-floor apartment. A bodyguard, for heaven's sake, a burly guy in a dark suit who could have passed for a Secret Service employee. She stifled the urge to scream in frustration.

Shannon flung herself out of the Escalade before it came to a complete stop, desperate to see her child, to get inside her tiny apartment in hopes that life would somehow return to normal. Tony couldn't be serious about her packing up to go away with him. He was just using this to try to get back together again.

Although what did a *prince* want with her?

At least there weren't any reporters in the parking lot. The neighbors all seemed to be inside for the evening or out enjoying their own party plans. She'd chosen the large complex for the anonymity it offered. Multiple three-story buildings filled the corner block, making it difficult to tell one apartment from another in the stretches of yellow units with tiny white balconies. At the center of it all, there was a pool and tiny playground, the only luxuries she'd allowed herself. She might not be able to give Kolby a huge yard, but he would have an outdoor place to play.

Now she had to start the search for a haven all over again.

"Here," she said as she thrust her purse toward him, her keys in her hand, "please carry this so I can unlock the door."

He extended his arm, her hobo bag dangling from his big fist. "Uh, sure."

"This is not the time to freak out over holding a woman's purse." She fumbled for the correct key.

"Shannon, I'm here for you. For you and your handbag."

She glanced back sharply. "Don't mock me."

"I thought you enjoyed my sense of humor."

Hadn't she thought just the same thing earlier? How could she say good-bye to Tony—he would never be Antonio to her—forever? Her feet slowed on the walkway between the simple hedges, nowhere near as elaborate as the gardens of her old home with Nolan, but well maintained. The place was clean.

And safe.

Having Tony at her back provided an extra layer of protection, she had to admit. After he'd made his shocking demand that she pack, he'd pulled out his phone and began checking in with his lawyer. From what she could tell hearing one side of the conversation, the news was spreading fast, with no indication of how the Global Intruder's people had cracked his cover. Tony didn't lose his temper or even curse.

But her normally lighthearted lover definitely wasn't smiling.

She ignored the soft note of regret spreading through her for all she would leave behind—this place. *Tony*. He strode alongside her silently, the outside lights casting his shadow over hers intimately, moving, tangling the two together as they walked.

Stopping at her unit three doors down from the corner, Tony exchanged low words with the guard while she slid the key into the lock with shaking hands. She pushed her way inside and ran smack into the babysitter already trying to open up for her. The college senior was majoring in elementary education and lived in the same complex. There might only be seven years between her and the girl in a concert T-shirt, but Shannon couldn't help but feel her own university days spent studying to be a teacher happened eons ago.

Shannon forced herself to stay calm. "Courtney, thanks for calling me. Where's Kolby?"

The sitter studied her with undisguised curiosity— who could blame her?—and pointed down the narrow hall toward the living room. "He's asleep on the couch. I thought it might be better to keep him with me in case any reporters started showing up outside or something." She hitched her bulging backpack onto one shoulder. "I don't think they would stake out his window, but ya never know. Right?"

"Thank you, Courtney. You did exactly the right thing." She angled down the hall to peek in on Kolby.

Her three-year-old son slept curled on the imported leather sofa, one of the few pieces that hadn't been sold to pay off debts. Kolby had poked a hole in the armrest with a fountain pen just before the estate sale. Shannon had strapped duct tape over the tear, grateful for one less piece of furniture to buy to start her new life.

Every penny she earned needed to be tucked away for

emergencies. Kolby counted on her, her sweet baby boy in his favorite Thomas the Tank Engine pj's, matching blanket held up to his nose. His blond hair was tousled and spiking, still damp from his bath. She could almost smell the baby-powder sweetness from across the room.

Sagging against the archway with relief, she turned back to Courtney. "I need to pay you."

Shannon took back her hobo bag from Tony and tunneled through frantically, dropping her wallet. Change clanked on the tile floor.

What would a three-year-old think if he saw his mother's face in some news report? Or Tony's, for that matter? The two had only met briefly a few times, but Kolby knew he was Mama's friend. She scooped the coins into a pile, picking at quarters and dimes.

Tony cupped her shoulder. "I've got it. Go ahead and be with your son."

She glanced up sharply, her nerves too raw to take the reminder of how he'd offered her financial help mere moments after sex last weekend. "I can pay my own way."

Holding up his hands, he backed away.

"Fine, Shannon. I'll sit with Kolby." He cautioned her with a look not to mention their plans to pack and leave.

Duh. Not that she planned to follow all *his* dictates, but the fewer who knew their next move the better for avoiding the press and anyone else who might profit from tracking their moves. Even the best of friends could be bought off.

Speaking of payoffs… "Thank you for calling me so quickly." She peeled off an extra twenty and tried not to wince as she said goodbye to ice cream for the month. She usually traded babysitting with another flat-broke single mom in the building when needed for work and dates.

Courtney was only her backup, which she couldn't—and didn't—use often. "I appreciate your help."

Shaking her head, Courtney took the money and passed back the extra twenty. "You don't need to give me all that, Mrs. Crawford. I was only doing my job. And I'm not gonna talk to the reporters. I'm not the kind of person who would sell your story or something."

"Really," Shannon urged as she folded the cash back into her hand, "I want you to have it."

Tony filled the archway. "The guard outside will walk you home, just to make sure no one bothers you."

"Thanks, Mr. Castillo. Um, I mean…" Courtney stuffed the folded bills into her back pocket, the college coed eyeing him up and down with a new awareness. "Mr. Medina… Sir? I don't what to call you."

"Castillo is fine."

"Right, uh, bye." Her face flushed, she spun on her glitter flip-flops and took off.

Shannon pushed the door closed, sliding the bolt and chain. Locking her inside with Tony in a totally quiet apartment. She slumped back and stared down the hallway, the ten feet shrinking even more with the bulk of his shoulders spanning the arch. Light from the cheap brown lamp glinted off the curl in his black hair.

No wonder Courtney had been flustered. He wasn't just a prince, but a fine-looking, one-hundred-percent *man*. The kind with strong hands that could finesse their way over a woman's body with a sweet tenderness that threatened to buckle her knees from just remembering. Had it only been a week since they'd made love in his mammoth jetted tub? God knows she ached as if she'd been without him for months.

Even acknowledging it was wrong with her mind, her body still wanted him.

* * *

Tony wanted her.

In his arms.

In his bed.

And most of all, he wanted her back in his SUV, heading away from here. He needed to use any methods of persuasion possible and convince her to come to his house. Even if the press located his home address, they wouldn't get past the gates and security. So how to convince Shannon? He stared down the short tiled hallway at her.

Awareness flared in her eyes. The same slam of attraction he felt now and the first time he'd seen her five months ago when he'd stopped by after a call to play cards. Vernon had mentioned hiring a new waitress but Tony hadn't thought much of it—until he met her.

When Tony asked about her, the old guy said he didn't know much about Shannon other than her crook of a husband had committed suicide rather than face a jury. Shannon and her boy had been left behind, flat broke. She'd worked at a small diner for a year and a half before that and Vernon had hired her on a hunch. Vernon and his softie heart.

Tony stared at her now every bit as intently as he had that first time she'd brought him his order. Something about her blue-gray eyes reminded him of the ocean sky just before a storm. Tumultuous. Interesting.

A challenge. He'd been without a challenge for too long. Building a business from nothing had kept him charged up for years. What next?

Then he'd seen her.

He'd spent his life smiling his way through problems and deals, and for the first time he'd found someone who saw past his bull. Was it the puzzle that tugged him? If so, he wasn't any closer to solving the mystery of Shannon.

Every day she confused him more, which made him want her more.

Pushing away from the door, she strode toward him, efficiently, no hip swish, just even, efficient steps. Then she walked out of her shoes, swiping one foot behind her to kick them to rest against the wall. No shoes in the house. She'd told him that the two times he'd been allowed over her threshold for no more than fifteen minutes. Any liaisons between them had been at his bayside mansion or a suite near the restaurant. He didn't really expect anything to happen here with her son around, even asleep.

And given the look on her face, she was more likely to pitch him out. Better to circumvent the boot.

"I'll stay with your son while you pack." He removed his shoes and stepped deeper into her place, not fancy, the sparse generic sort of a furnished space in browns and tan—except for the expensive burgundy leather sofa with a duct-taped *X* on the armrest.

Her lips thinned. "About packing, we need to discuss that further."

"What's to talk about?" He accepted their relationship was still on hold, but the current problems with his identity needed to be addressed. "Your porch will be full by morning."

"I'll check into a hotel."

With the twenty dollars and fifty-two cents she had left in her wallet? He prayed she wasn't foolish enough to use a credit card. Might as well phone in her location to the news stations.

"We can talk about where you'll stay *after* you pack."

"You sound like a broken record, Tony."

"*You're* calling *me* stubborn?"

Their standoff continued, neither of them touching, but he was all too aware of her scrubbed fresh scent.

Shannon, the whole place, carried an air of some kind of floral cleaner. The aroma somehow calmed and stirred at the same time, calling to mind holding her after a mind-bending night of sex. She never stayed over until morning, but for an hour or so after, she would doze against his chest. He would breathe in the scent of her and him and *them* blended together.

His nose flared.

Her pupils widened.

She stumbled back, her chest rising faster. "I do need to change my clothes. Are you sure you'll be all right with Kolby?"

It was no secret the couple of times he'd met the boy, Kolby hadn't warmed up to him. Nothing seemed to work, not ice cream or magic coin tricks. Tony figured maybe the boy was still missing his father.

That jerk had left Shannon bankrupt and vulnerable. "I can handle it. Take all the time you need."

"Thank you. I'm only going to change clothes though. No packing yet. We'll have to talk more first, Tony—um, Antonio."

"I prefer to be called *Tony*." He liked the sound of it on her tongue.

"Okay...Tony." She spun on her heel and headed toward her bedroom.

Her steps still efficient, albeit faster, were just speedy enough to bring a slight swing to her slim hips in the pencil-straight skirt. Thoughts of peeling it down and off her beautiful body would have to wait until she had the whole Antonio/Tony issue sorted out.

If only she could accept that he'd called himself Tony Castillo almost longer than he'd remembered being Antonio Medina.

He even had the paperwork to back up the Castillo

name. Creating another persona hadn't been that difficult, especially once he'd saved enough to start his first business. From then on, all transactions were shuttled through the company. Umbrella corporations. Living in plain sight. His plan had worked fine until someone, somehow had pierced the new identities he and his brothers had built. In fact, he needed to call his brothers, who he spoke to at most a couple of times a year. But they might have insights.

They needed a plan.

He reached inside his jacket for his iPhone and ducked into the dining area where he could see the child but wouldn't wake him. He thumbed the seven key on his speed dial...and Carlos's voice mail picked up. Tony disconnected without leaving a message and pressed the eight key.

"Speak to me, my brother." Duarte Medina's voice came through the phone. They didn't talk often, but these weren't normal circumstances.

"I assume you know." He toyed with one of Shannon's hair bands on the table.

"Impossible to miss."

"Where's Carlos? He's not picking up." Tony fell back into their clipped shorthand. They'd only had each other growing up and now circumstances insisted they stay apart. Did his brothers have that same feeling, like they'd lost a limb?

"His secretary said he got paged for an emergency surgery. He'll be at least another couple of hours. Apparently Carlos found out as he was scrubbing in, but you know our brother." Duarte, the middle son, tended to play messenger with their father. The three brothers spoke and met when they could, but there were so many crap memories from their childhood, those reunions became further apart.

Tony scooped up the brown band, a lone long strand

of her blond hair catching the light. "When a patient calls…"

"Right."

It could well be hours before they heard from Carlos, given the sort of painstaking reconstructive surgeries he performed on children. "Any idea how this exploded?"

His brother hissed a long angry curse. "The Global Intruder got a side-view picture of me while I was visiting our sister."

Their half sister Eloisa, their father's daughter from an affair shortly after they had escaped to the States. Enrique had still been torn up with grief from losing his wife… not to mention the guilt. But apparently not so torn up and remorseful he couldn't hop into bed with someone else. The woman had gone on to marry another man who'd raised her daughter as his own.

Tony had only met his half sister once as a teen, a few years before he'd left the island compound. She'd only been seven at the time. Now she'd married into a high-profile family jam-packed with political influence and a fat portfolio. Could she be at fault for bringing the media down on their heads for some free PR for her new in-laws? Duarte seemed to think she wanted anonymity as much as the rest of them. But could he have misjudged her?

"Why were you visiting Eloisa?" Tony tucked the band into his pocket.

"Family business. It doesn't matter now. Her in-laws were there. Eloisa's sister-in-law—a senator's wife—slipped on the dock. I kept her from falling into the water. Some damn female reporter in a tree with a telephoto lens caught the mishap. Which shouldn't have mattered, since Senator Landis and his wife were the focus of the picture. I still don't know how the photographer pegged me from a side view, but there it is. And I'm sorry for bringing this crap down on you."

Duarte hadn't done anything wrong. They couldn't live in a bubble. In the back of Tony's mind, he'd always known it was just a matter of time until the cover story blew up in their faces. He'd managed to live away from the island anonymously for fourteen years, his two older brothers even longer.

But there was always the hope that maybe he could stay a step ahead. Be his own man. Succeed on his own merits. "We've all been caught in a picture on occasion. We're not vampires. It's just insane that she was able to make the connection. Perfect storm of bad luck."

"What are your plans for dealing with this perfect storm?"

"Lock down tight while I regroup. Let me know when you hear from Carlos."

Ending the call, Tony strode back into the living room, checked on Kolby—still snoozing hard—and dropped to the end of the sofa to read messages, his in-box already full again. By the time Tony scrolled through emails that told him nothing new, he logged on to the internet for a deeper peek. And winced. Rumors were rampant.

That his father had died of malaria years ago—false.

Supposition that Carlos had plastic surgery—again, false.

Speculation that Duarte had joined a Tibetan monastery—definitely false.

And then there were the stories about him and Shannon, which actually happened to be true. The whole "Monarch's Mistress" was really growing roots out there in cyberspace. Guilt kicked him in the gut that Shannon would suffer this kind of garbage because of him. The media feeding frenzy would only grow, and before long they would stir up all the crap about her thief of a dead husband. He tucked away his phone in disgust.

"That bad?" Shannon asked from the archway.

She'd changed into jeans and a simple blue tank top. Her silky blond hair glided loosely down her shoulders, straight except for a slight crimped ring where she'd bound it up on her head for work. She didn't look much older than the babysitter, except in her weary—wary—eyes.

Leaning back, he extended his legs, leather creaking as he stayed on the sofa so as not to spook her. "The internet is exploding. My lawyers and my brothers' lawyers are all looking into it. Hopefully we'll have the leak plugged soon and start some damage control. But we can't stuff the genie back into the bottle."

"I'm not going away with you." She perched a fist on one shapely hip.

"This isn't going to die down." He kept his voice even and low, reasonable. The stakes were too important for all of them. "The reporters will swarm you by morning, if not sooner. Your babysitter will almost inevitably cave in to one of those gossip rag offers. Your friends will sell photos of the two of us together. There's a chance people could use Kolby to get to me."

"Then we're through, you and I." She reached for her sleeping son on the sofa, smoothing his hair before sliding a hand under his shoulders as if to scoop him up.

Tony touched her arm lightly, stopping her. "Hold on before you settle him into his room." As far as Tony was concerned, they would be back in his Escalade in less than ten minutes. "Do you honestly think anyone's going to believe the breakup is for real? The timing will seem too convenient."

She sagged onto the arm of the sofa, right over the silver X. "We ended things last weekend."

Like hell. "Tell that to the papers and see if they believe you. The truth doesn't matter to these people. They probably printed photos of an alien baby last week. Pleading a breakup isn't going to buy you any kind of freedom from their interest."

"I know I need to move away from Galveston." She glanced around her sparsely decorated apartment, two pictures of Kolby the only personal items. "I've accepted that."

There wouldn't be much packing to do.

"They'll find you."

She studied him through narrowed eyes. "How do I know you're not just using this as an excuse to get back together?"

Was he? An hour ago, he would have done anything to get into her bed again. While the attraction hadn't diminished, since his cover was blown, he had other concerns that overshadowed everything else. He needed to determine the best way to inoculate her from the toxic fallout that came from associating with Medinas. One thing for certain, he couldn't risk her striking out on her own.

"You made it clear where we stand last weekend. I get that. You want nothing to do with me or my money." He didn't move closer, wasn't going to crowd her. The draw between them filled the space separating them just fine on its own. "We had sex together. Damn good sex. But that's over now. Neither one of us ever asked for or expected more."

Her gaze locked with his, the room silent but for their breathing and the light snore of the sleeping child. Kolby. Another reminder of why they needed to stay in control.

In fact, holding back made the edge sharper. He skimmed his knuckles along her collarbone, barely touching. A week ago, that pale skin had worn the rasp of his beard. She didn't move closer, but she didn't back away, either.

Shannon blinked first, her long lashes sweeping closed while she swallowed hard. "What am I supposed to do?"

More than anything he wanted to gather her up and tell her everything would be okay. He wouldn't allow anything less. But he also wouldn't make shallow promises.

Twenty-seven years ago, when they'd been leaving San Rinaldo on a moonless night, his father had assured them everything would be fine. They would be reunited soon.

His father had been so very wrong.

Tony focused on what he could assure. "A lot has happened in a few hours. We need to take a step back for damage assessment tonight at my home, where there are security gates, alarms, guards watching and surveillance cameras."

"And after tonight?"

"We'll let the press think we are a couple, still deep in that affair." He indulged himself in one lengthy, heated eye-stroke of her slim, supple body. "Then we'll stage a more public breakup later, on our terms, when we've prepared a backup plan."

She exhaled a shaky breath. "That makes sense."

"Meanwhile, my number one priority is shielding you and Kolby." He sifted through options, eliminating one idea after another until he was left with only a single alternative.

Her hand fell to rest on her sleeping son's head. "How do you intend to do that?"

"By taking you to the safest place I know." A place he'd vowed never to return. "Tomorrow, we're going to visit my father."

Three

"Visit your father?" Shannon asked in total shock. Had Tony lost his mind? "The King of San Rinaldo? You've got to be kidding."

"I'm completely serious." He stared back at her from the far end of the leather sofa, her sleeping son between them.

Resisting Tony had been tough enough this past week just knowing he was in the same town. How much more difficult would it be with him in the same house for one night much less days on end? God, she wanted to run. She bit the inside of her lip to keep from blurting out something she would regret later. Sorting through her options could take more time than they appeared to have.

Kolby wriggled restlessly, hugging his comfort blanket tighter. Needing a moment to collect her thoughts and her resolve, she scooped up her son.

"Tony, we'll have to put this discussion on hold." She

cradled her child closer and angled down the hall, ever aware of a certain looming prince at her back. "Keep the lights off, please."

Shadows playing tag on the ceiling, she lowered Kolby into the red caboose bed they'd picked out together when she moved into the apartment. She'd been trying so hard to make up for all her son had lost. As if there was some way to compensate for the loss of his father, the loss of security. Shannon pressed a kiss to his forehead, inhaling his precious baby-shampoo smell.

When she turned back, she found Tony waiting in the doorway, determination stamped on his square jaw. Well, she could be mighty resolute too, especially when it came to her son. Shannon closed the curtains before she left the room and stepped into the narrow hall.

She shut the door quietly behind her. "You have to know your suggestion is outrageous."

"The whole situation is outrageous, which calls for extraordinary measures."

"Hiding out with a king? That's definitely what I would call extraordinary." She pulled off her glasses and pinched the bridge of her nose.

Before Nolan's death she'd worn contacts, but couldn't afford the extra expense now. How much longer until she would grow accustomed to glasses again?

She stared at Tony, his face clear up close, everything in the distance blurred. "Do you honestly think I would want to expose myself, not to mention Kolby, to more scrutiny by going to your father's? Why not just hide out at your place as we originally discussed?"

God, had she just agreed to stay with him indefinitely?

"My house is secure, up to a point. People will figure out where I live and they'll deduce that you're with me.

There's only one place I can think of where no one can get to us."

Frustration buzzed in her brain. "Seems like their telephoto lenses reach everywhere."

"The press still hasn't located my father's home after years of trying."

But she thought… "Doesn't he live in Argentina?"

He studied her silently, the wheels almost visibly turning in his broad forehead. Finally, he shook his head quickly.

"No. We only stopped off there to reorganize after escaping San Rinaldo." He adjusted his watch, the only nervous habit she'd ever observed in him. "My father did set up a compound there and paid a small, trusted group of individuals to make it look inhabited. Most of them also escaped San Rinaldo with us. People assumed we were there with them."

What extreme lengths and expense their father had gone to. But then wasn't she willing to do anything to protect Kolby? She felt a surprise connection to the old king she'd never met. "Why are you telling me this much if it's such a closely guarded secret?"

He cupped her shoulder, his touch heavy and familiar, *stirring*. "Because it's that important I persuade you."

Resisting the urge to lean into him was tougher with each stroke of his thumb against the sensitive curve of her neck. "Where *does* he live then?"

"I can't tell you that much," he said, still touching and God, it made her mad that she didn't pull away.

"Yet you expect me to just pack up my child and follow you there." She gripped his wrist and moved away his seductive touch.

"I detect a note of skepticism in your voice." He shoved his hands in his pockets.

"A note? Try a whole freaking symphony, Tony." The sense of betrayal swelled inside her again, larger and larger until it pushed bitter words out. "Why should I trust you? Especially now?"

"Because you don't have anyone else or they would have already been helping you."

The reality deflated her. She only had a set of in-laws who didn't want anything to do with her or Kolby since they blamed her for their son's downfall. She was truly alone.

"How long would we be there?"

"Just until my attorneys can arrange for a restraining order against certain media personnel. I realize that restraining orders don't always work, but having one will give us a stronger legal case if we need it. It's one thing to stalk, but it's another to stalk and violate a restraining order. And I'll want to make sure you have top-of-the-line security installed at your new home. That should take about a week, two at the most."

Shannon fidgeted with her glasses. "How would we get there?"

"By plane." He thumbed the face of his watch clean again.

That meant it must be far away. "Forget it. You are not going to isolate me that way, cut me off from the world. It's the equivalent of kidnapping me and my son."

"Not if you agree to go along." He edged closer, the stretch of his hard muscled shoulders blocking out the light filtering from the living area. "People in the military get on planes all the time without knowing their destination."

She tipped her chin upward, their faces inches apart. Close enough to feel his heat. Close enough to kiss.

Too close for her own good. "Last time I checked, I wasn't wearing a uniform." Her voice cracked ever so slightly. "I didn't sign on for this."

"I know, Shanny...." He stroked a lock of her hair intimately. "I *am* sorry for all this is putting you through, and I will do my best to make the next week as easy for you as possible."

The sincerity of his apology soothed the ragged edges of her nerves. It had been a long week without him. She'd been surprised by how much she had missed his spontaneous dates and late-night calls. His bold kisses and intimate caresses. She couldn't lie to herself about how much he affected her on both an emotional and physical level. Otherwise this mess with his revealed past wouldn't hurt her so deeply.

Her hand clenched around her glasses. He gently slid them from her hand and hooked them on the front of her shirt. The familiarity of the gesture kicked her heart rate up a notch.

Swaying toward him, she flattened her hands to his chest, not sure if she wanted to push him away or pull him nearer. Thick longing filled the sliver of space between them. An answering awareness widened his pupils, pushing and thinning the dark brown of his eyes.

He lowered his head closer, closer still until his mouth hovered over hers. Heated breaths washed over her, stirring even hotter memories and warm languid longing. She'd thought the pain of Nolan's deceit had left her numb for life...until she saw Tony.

"Mama?"

The sound of her son calling out from his room jolted her back to reality. And not only her. Tony's face went from seductive to intent in a heartbeat. He pulled the door open just as Kolby ran through and into his mother's arms.

"Mama, Mama, Mama..." He buried his face in her neck. "Monster in my window!"

* * *

Tony shot through the door and toward the window in the child's room, focused, driven and mentally kicking himself for letting himself be distracted.

He barked over his shoulder, "Stay in the hall while I take a look."

It could be nothing, but he'd been taught at a young age the importance of never letting down his guard. Adrenaline firing, he jerked the window open and scanned the tiny patch of yard.

Nothing. Just a Big Wheel lying on its side and a swing dangling lazily from a lone tree.

Maybe it was only a nightmare. This whole blast from the past had him seeing bogeymen from his own childhood, too. Tony pushed the window down again and pulled the curtains together.

Shannon stood in the door, her son tucked against her. "I could have sworn I closed the curtains."

Kolby peeked up. "I opened 'em when I heard-ed the noise."

And maybe this kid's nightmare was every bit as real as his own had been. On the off chance the boy was right, he had to check. "I'm going outside. The guard will stay here with you."

She cupped the back of her child's head. "I already warned the guard. I wasn't leaving you to take care of the 'monster' by yourself."

Dread kinked cold and tight in his gut. What if something had happened to her when she had stepped outside to speak to the guard? He held in the angry words, not wanting to upset her son.

But he became more determined by the second to persuade her and the child to leave Galveston with him.

"Let's hope it was nothing but a tree branch. Right, kiddo?"

Tony started toward the door just as his iPhone rang. He glanced at the ID and saw the guard's number. He thumbed the speaker phone button. "Yes?"

"Got him," the guard said. "A teenager from the next complex over was trying to snap some pictures on his cell phone. I've already called the police."

A sigh shuddered through Shannon, and she hugged her son closer, and God, how Tony wanted to comfort her.

However, the business of taking care of her safety came first. "Keep me posted if there are any red flags when they interview the trespasser. Good work. Thanks."

He tucked his phone back into his jacket, his heart almost hammering out of his chest at the close call. This could have been worse. He knew too well from past experience how bad it could have been.

And apparently so did Shannon. Her wide blue eyes blinked erratically as she looked from corner to corner, searching shadows.

To hell with giving her distance. He wrapped an arm around her shoulders until she leaned on him ever so slightly. The soft press of her against him felt damn right in a day gone wrong.

Then she squeezed her eyes closed and straightened. "Okay, you win."

"Win what?"

"We'll go to your home tonight."

A hollow victory, since fear rather than desire motivated her, but he wasn't going to argue. "And tomorrow?"

"We'll discuss that in morning. Right now, just take us to your house."

* * *

Tony's Galveston house could only be called a mansion.

The imposing size of the three-story structure washed over Shannon every time they drove through the scrolled iron gates. How Kolby could sleep through all of this boggled her mind, but when they'd convinced him the "monster" was gone—thanks to the guard—Kolby had been all yawns again. Once strapped into the car seat in the back of Tony's Escalade, her son had been out like a light in five minutes.

If only her own worries could be as easily shaken off. She had to think logically, but fears for Kolby nagged her. Nolan had stolen so much more than money. He'd robbed her of the ability to feel safe, just before he took the coward's way out.

Two acres of manicured lawn stretched ahead of her in the moonlight. The estate was intimidating during the day, and all the more ominously gothic at night with shadowy edges encroaching. It was one thing to visit the place for a date.

It was another to take shelter here, to pack suitcases and accept his help.

She'd lived in a large house with Nolan, four thousand square feet, but she could have fit two of those homes inside Tony's place. In the courtyard, a concrete horse fountain was illuminated, glowing in front of the burgundy stucco house with brown trim so dark it was almost black. His home showcased the Spanish architecture prevalent in Texas. Knowing his true heritage now, she could see why he would have been drawn to this area.

Silently he guided the SUV into the garage, finally safe and secure from the outside world. For how long?

He unstrapped Kolby from the seat and she didn't argue. Her son was still sleeping anyway. The way Tony's big hands managed the small buckles and shuffled the sleeping child onto his shoulder with such competence touched her heart as firmly as any hothouse full of roses.

Trailing him with a backpack of toy trains and trucks, she dimly registered the house that had grown familiar after their dates to restaurants, movies and the most amazing concerts. Her soul, so starved for music, gobbled up every note.

Her first dinner at his home had been a five-course catered meal with a violinist. She could almost hear the echoing strains bouncing lightly off the high-beamed ceiling, down to the marble floor, swirling along the inlay pattern to twine around her.

Binding her closer to him. They hadn't had sex that night, but she'd known then it was inevitable.

That first time, Tony had been thoughtful enough to send out to a different restaurant than his favored Vernon's, guessing accurately that when a person worked eight hours a day in one eating establishment, the food there lost its allure.

He'd opted for Italian cuisine. The meal and music and elegance had been so far removed from paper plate dinners of nuggets and fries. While she adored her son and treasured every second with him, she couldn't help but be wooed by grown-up time to herself.

Limited time as she'd never spent the night here. Until now.

She followed Tony up the circular staircase, hand on the crafted iron banister. The sight of her son sleeping so limp and relaxed against Tony brought a lump to her throat again.

The tenderness she felt seeing him hold her child reminded her how special this new man in her life was. She'd chosen him so carefully after Nolan had died, seeing

Tony's innate strength and honor. Was she really ready to throw that away?

He stopped at the first bedroom, a suite decorated in hunter green with vintage maps framed on the walls. Striding through the sitting area to the next door, he flipped back the brocade spread and set her son in the middle of the high bed.

Quietly, she put a chair on either side as a makeshift bed rail, then tucked the covers over his shoulders. She kissed his little forehead and inhaled his baby-fresh scent. Her child.

The enormity of how their lives had changed tonight swelled inside her, pushing stinging tears to the surface. Tony's hand fell to rest on her shoulder and she leaned back….

Holy crap.

She jolted away. How easily she fell into old habits around him. "I didn't mean…"

"I know." His hand fell away and tucked into his pocket. "I'll carry up your bags in a minute. I gave the house staff the night off."

She followed him, just to keep their conversation soft, not because she wasn't ready to say good-night. "I thought you trusted them."

"I do. To a point. It's also easier for security to protect the house with fewer people inside." He gestured into the sitting area. "I heard what you said about feeling cut off from the world going to my father's and I understand."

His empathy slipped past her defenses when they were already on shaky ground being here in his house again. Remembering all the times they'd made love under this very roof, she could almost smell the bath salts from last weekend. And with him being so understanding on top of everything else…

He'd lied. She needed to remember that.

"I realize I have to do what's right for Kolby." She sagged onto the striped sofa, her legs folding from an emotional and exhausting night. "It scares the hell out of me how close a random teenager already got to my child, and we're only a couple of hours into this mess. It makes me ill to think about what someone with resources could do."

"My brothers and I have attorneys. They'll look into pressing charges against the teen." He sat beside her with a casual familiarity of lovers.

Remember the fight. Not the bath salts. She inched toward the armrest. "Let me know what the attorneys' fees are, please."

"They're on retainer. Those lawyers also help us communicate with each other. My attorney will know we're going to see my father if you're worried about making sure someone is aware of your plans."

Someone under his employ, all of this bought with Tony's money that she'd rejected a few short days ago. And she couldn't think of any other way. "You trust this man, your lawyer?"

"I have to." The surety in his voice left little room for doubt. "There are some transactions that can't be avoided no matter how much we want to sever ties with the past."

A darker note in his voice niggled at her. "Are you talking about yourself now?"

He shrugged, broad shoulders rippling the fabric of his fine suit.

Nuh-uh. She wasn't giving up that easily. She'd trusted so much of her life to this man, only to find he'd misled her.

Now she needed something tangible, something honest from him to hold on to. Something to let her know if that honor and strength she'd perceived in him was real. "You said you didn't want to break off our relationship. If that's true, this would be a really good time to open up a little."

Angling toward her, Tony's knee pressed against hers, his eyes heating to molten dark. "Are you saying we're good again?"

"I'm saying…" She cleared her throat that had suddenly gone cottony dry. "Maybe I could see my way clear to forgiving you if I knew more about you."

He straightened, his eyes sharp. "What do you want to know?"

"Why Galveston?"

"Do you surf?"

What the hell? She watched the walls come up in his eyes. She could almost feel him distancing himself from her. "Tony, I'm not sure how sharing a *Surf's Up* moment is going to make things all better here."

"But have you ever been surfing?" He gestured, his hands riding imaginary waves. "The Atlantic doesn't offer as wild a ride as the Pacific, but it gets the job done, especially in Spain. Something to do with the atmospheric pressure coming down from the U.K. I still remember the swells tubing." He curled his fingers around into the cresting circle of a wave.

"You're a *surfer?*" She tried to merge the image of the sleek business shark with the vision of him carefree on a board. And instead an image emerged of his abandon when making love. Her breasts tingled and tightened, awash in the sensation of sea spray and Tony all over her skin.

"I've always been fascinated with waves."

"Even when you were in San Rinaldo." The picture of him began to make more sense. "It's an island country, right?"

She'd always thought the nautical art on his walls was tied into his shipping empire. Now she realized the affinity for such pieces came from living on an island. So much about him made sense.

His surfing hand soared to rest on the gold flecked globe beside the sofa. Was it her imagination or was the gloss dimmer over the coast of Spain? As if he'd rubbed his finger along that area more often, taking away the sheen over time.

He spun the globe. "I thought you didn't know much about the Medinas."

"I researched you on Google on my phone while we were driving over." Concrete info had been sparse compared to all the crazy gossip floating about, but there were some basics. Three sons. A monarch father. A mother who'd been killed as they were escaping. Her heart squeezed thinking of him losing a parent so young, not much older than Kolby.

She pulled a faltering smile. "There weren't any surfer pictures among the few images that popped up."

Only a couple of grainy formal family portraits of three young boys with their parents, everyone happy. Some earlier photos of King Enrique looking infinitely regal.

"We scrubbed most pictures after we escaped and regrouped." His lighthearted smile contrasted with the darker hue deepening his eyes. "The internet wasn't active in those days."

The extent of his rebuilding shook her to her shoes. She'd thought she had it rough leaving Louisiana after her husband's arrest and death. How tragic to have your past wiped away. The enormity of what had happened to his family, of how he'd lived since then, threatened to overwhelm her.

How could she not ache over all he'd been through? "I saw that your mother died when I read up on your past. I'm so sorry."

He waved away her sympathy. "When we got to…where my father lives now, things were isolated. But at least we still had the ocean. Out on the waves, I could forget about everything else."

Plowing a hand through his hair, he stared just past her, obviously locked in some deep memories. She sensed she was close, so close to the something she needed to reassure her that placing herself and her son in his care would be wise, even if there weren't gossip seekers sifting through her trash.

She rested her hand on his arm. "What are you thinking?"

"I thought you might like to learn next spring. Unless you're already a pro."

"Not hardly." Spring was a long way off, a huge commitment she wasn't anywhere near ready to make to anyone. The thought of climbing on a wave made her stomach knot almost as much as being together that long. "Thanks for the offer, but I'll pass."

"Scared?" He skimmed his knuckles over her collarbone, and just that fast the sea-spray feel tingled through her again.

"Hell, yes. Scared of getting hurt."

His hand stilled just above her thumping heart. Want crackled in the air. Hers? Or his? She wasn't sure. Probably equal measures from both of them. That had never been in question. And too easily he could draw her in again. Learning more about him wasn't wise after all, not tonight.

She pulled away, her arms jerky, her whole body out of whack. She needed Tony's lightness now. Forget about serious peeks into each other's vulnerable pasts. "No surfing for me. Ever try taking care of a toddler with a broken leg?"

"When did you break your leg?" His eyes narrowed. "Did he hurt you? Your husband?"

How had Tony made that leap so quickly?

"Nolan was a crook and a jerk, but he never raised a hand to me." She shivered, not liking the new direction their conversation had taken at all. This was supposed to teach her more about him. Not the other way around. "Do we have to drag more baggage into this?"

"If it's true."

"I told you. He didn't abuse me." Not physically. "Having a criminal for a husband is no picnic. Knowing I missed the signs… Wondering if I let myself be blind to it because I enjoyed the lifestyle… I don't even know where to start in answering those questions for myself."

She slumped, suddenly exhausted, any residual adrenaline fizzling out. Her head fell back.

"Knowing you as I do, I find it difficult to believe you would ever choose the easy path." Tony thumbed just below her eyes where undoubtedly dark circles were all but tattooed on her face. "It's been a long day. You should get some rest. If you want, I'll tuck you in," he said with a playful wink.

She found the old Tony much easier to deal with than the new. "You're teasing, of course."

"Maybe…" And just that fast the light in his eyes flamed hotter, intense. "Shanny, I would hold you all night if you would let me. I would make sure no one dared threaten you or your son again."

And she wanted to let him do just that. But she'd allowed herself to depend on a man before… "If you hold me, we both know I won't get any rest, and while I'll have pleasure tonight, I'll be sorry tomorrow. Don't you think we have enough wrong between us right now without adding another regret to the mix?"

"Okay…." Tony gave her shoulder a final squeeze and stood. "I'll back off."

Shannon pushed to her feet alongside him, her hands fisted at her sides to keep from reaching for him. "I'm still mad over being kept in the dark, but I appreciate all the damage control."

"I owe you that much and more." He kissed her lightly on the lips without touching her anywhere else, lingering long enough to remind her of the reasons they clicked. Her breath hitched and it was all she could do not to haul him in closer for a firmer, deeper connection.

Pulling back, he started toward the door.

"Tony?" Was that husky voice really hers?

He glanced over his shoulder. So easily she could take the physical comfort waiting only a few feet away in his arms. But she had to keep her head clear. She had to hold strong to carve out an independent life for her and her son and that meant drawing clear boundaries.

"Just because I might be able to forgive you doesn't mean you're welcome in my bed again."

Four

She wasn't in her own bed.

Shannon wrestled with the tenacious grip of her shadowy nightmare, tough as hell to do when she couldn't figure out where she was. The ticking grandfather clock, the feel of the silky blanket around her, none of it was familiar. And then a hint of sandalwood scent teased her nose a second before…

"Hey." Tony's voice rumbled through the dark. "It's okay. I'm here."

Her heart jumped. She bolted upright, the cashmere afghan twisting around her legs and waist. Blinking fast, she struggled to orient herself to the surroundings so different from her apartment, but the world blurred in front of her from the dark and her own crummy eyesight. Shannon pressed her hands to the cushiony softness of a sofa and everything came rushing back. She was at Tony's, in the sitting room outside where Kolby slept.

"It's okay," Tony continued to chant, squeezing her shoulder in his broad hand as he crouched beside the couch.

Swinging her feet to the ground, she gathered the haunting remnants of her nightmare. Shadows smoked through her mind, blending into a darker mass of memories from the night Nolan died, except Tony's face superimposed itself over that of her dead husband.

Nausea burned her throat. She swallowed back the bite of bile and the horror of her dream. "Sorry, if I woke you." Oh, God, her son. "Is Kolby all right?"

"Sleeping soundly."

"Thank goodness. I wouldn't want to frighten him." She took in Tony's mussed hair and hastily hauled on jeans. The top button was open and his chest was bare. Gulp. "I'm sorry for disturbing you."

"I wasn't asleep." He passed her glasses to her.

As she slid them on, his tattoo came into focus, a nautical compass on his arm. Looking closer she realized his hair was wet. She didn't want to think about him in the shower, a tiled spa cubicle they'd shared more than once. "It's been a tough night all around."

"Want to talk about what woke you up?"

"Not really." Not ever. To anyone. "I think my fear for Kolby ran wild in my sleep. Dreams are supposed to help work out problems, but sometimes, it seems they only make everything scarier."

"Ah, damn, Shanny, I'm sorry for this whole mess." He sat on the sofa and slid an arm around her shoulders.

She stiffened, then decided to hell with it all and leaned back against the hard wall of chest. With the nightmare so fresh in her mind, she couldn't scavenge the will to pull away. His arms banded around her in an instant and her head tucked under his chin. Somehow it was easier to accept this comfort when she didn't have to look in his eyes. She'd been alone with her bad dreams for so long. Was it wrong to take just a second's comfort from his arms roped so thick with muscles nothing could break through to her? She would be strong again in a minute.

The grandfather clock ticked away minutes as she stared at his hands linked over her stomach—at the lighter band of skin where his watch usually rested. "Thanks for coming in to check on us, especially so late."

"It can be disconcerting waking in an unfamiliar place alone." His voice vibrated against her back, only her thin nightshirt between them and his bare chest.

Another whiff of his freshly showered scent teased her nose with memories of steam-slicked bodies.

"I've been here at least a dozen times, but never in this room. It's a big house." They'd met five months ago, started dating two months later…had starting sleeping together four weeks ago. "Strange to think we've shared the shower, but I still haven't seen all of your home."

"We tended to get distracted once our feet hit the steps," he said drily.

True enough. They'd stayed downstairs on early dinner dates here, but once they'd ventured upstairs…they'd always headed straight for his suite.

"That first time together—" Shannon remembered was after an opera when her senses had been on overload and her hormones on hyperdrive from holding back "—I was scared to death."

The admission tumbled out before she could think, but somehow it seemed easier to share such vulnerabilities in the dark.

His muscles flexed against her, the bristle of hair on his arms teasing goose bumps along her skin. "The last thing I ever want to do is frighten you."

"It wasn't your fault. That night was a big leap of faith for me." The need to make him understand pushed past walls she'd built around herself. "Being with you then, it was my first time since Nolan."

He went completely still, not even breathing for four ticks of the clock before she felt his neck move with a swallow against her temple. "No one?"

"No one." Not only had Tony been her sole lover since Nolan, he'd been her second lover ever.

Her track record for picking men with secrets sucked.

His gusty sigh ruffled her hair. "I wish you would have told me."

"What would that have changed?"

"I would have been more…careful."

The frenzy of their first time stormed her mind with a barrage of images…their clothes fluttering to carpet the stairs on their way up. By the top of the steps they were naked, moonlight bathing his olive skin and casting shadows along the cut of muscles. Kissing against the wall soon had her legs wrapped around his waist and he was inside her. That one thrust had unfurled the tension into shimmering sensations and before the orgasm finished tingling all the way to the roots of her hair, he'd carried her to his room, her legs still around him. Again, she'd found release in bed with him, then a languid, leisurely completion while showering together.

Just remembering, an ache started low, throbbing between her legs. "You were great that night, and you know it." She swatted his hand lightly. "Now wipe the arrogant grin off your face."

"You can't see me." His voice sounded somber enough.

"Am I right, though?"

"Look at me and see."

She turned around and dared to peer up at him for the first time since he'd settled on the couch behind her. Her intense memories of that evening found an echo in his serious eyes far more moving than any smile.

Right now, it was hard to remember they weren't a couple anymore. "Telling you then would have made the event too serious."

Too important.

His offer to "help" her financially still loomed unresolved between them, stinging her even more than last weekend after the enormous secret he'd kept from her. Why couldn't they be two ordinary people who met at the park outside her apartment complex? What would it have been like to get to know Tony on neutral, normal ground? Would she have been able to see past the pain of her marriage?

She would never know.

"Shannon." His voice came out hoarse and hungry. "Are you okay to go back to sleep now? Because I need to leave."

His words splashed a chill over her heated thoughts. "Of course, you must have a lot to take care of with your family."

"You misunderstand. I *need* to leave, because you're killing me here with how much I've hurt you. And as if that wasn't enough to bring me to my knees, every time you move your head, the feel of your hair against my chest just about sends me over the edge." His eyes burned with a coal-hot determination. "I'll be damned before I do anything to break your trust again."

Before she could unscramble her thoughts, he slid his arms from her and ducked out the door as silently as he'd arrived. Colder than ever without the heat of Tony all around her, she hugged the blanket closer.

No worries about any more nightmares, because she was more than certain she wouldn't be able to go back to sleep.

By morning, Tony hadn't bothered turning down the covers on his bed. After leaving Shannon's room, he'd spent most of the night conferring with his lawyer and a security firm. Working himself into the ground to distract himself from how much he hurt from wanting her.

With a little luck and maneuvering, he could extend his week with her into two weeks. But bottom line, he *would* ensure her safety.

At five, he'd caught a catnap on the library sofa, jolting awake when Vernon called him from the front gate. He'd buzzed the retired sea captain through and rounded up breakfast.

His old friend deserved some answers.

Choosing a less formal dining area outside, he sat at the oval table on the veranda shaded by a lemon tree, Vernon beside him with a plate full of churros. Tony thumbed the edge of the hand-painted stoneware plate—a set he'd picked up from a local craftsman to support the dying art of the region.

Today of all days, he didn't want to think overlong on why he still ate his same childhood breakfast—deep fried strips of potato dough. His mother had always poured a thick rich espresso for herself and mugs of hot chocolate for her three sons, an informal ritual in their centuries-old castle that he now knew was anything but ordinary.

Vernon eyed him over the rim of his coffee cup. "So it's all true, what they're saying in the papers and on the internet?"

Absurd headlines scrolled through his memory, alongside reports that had been right on the money. "My brother's not a Tibetan monk, but the general gist of that first report from the Global Intruder is correct."

"You're a prince." He scrubbed a hand over his dropped jaw. "Well, hot damn. Always knew there was something special about you, boy."

He preferred to think anything "special" about him came from hard work rather than a genetic lottery win. "I hope you understand it wasn't my place to share the details with you."

"You have brothers and a father." He stirred a hefty dollop of milk into his coffee, clinking the spoon against the edges of the stoneware mug. "I get that you need to consider their privacy, as well."

"Thanks, I appreciate that."

He wished Shannon could see as much. He'd hoped bringing her here would remind her of all that had been good between them. Instead those memories had only come back to bite him on the ass when she'd told him that he was her first since her husband died. The revelation still sucker punched the air from his gut.

Where did they go from there? Hell if he knew, but at least he had more time to find out. Soon enough he would have her in his private jet that waited fueled and ready a mile away.

The older man set down his mug. "I respect that you gotta be your own man."

"Thank you again." He'd expected Vernon to be angry over the secrecy, had even been concerned over losing his friendship.

Vernon's respect meant a lot to him, as well as his advice. From day one when Tony had turned in his sparse job application, Vernon had treated him like a son, showing him the ropes. They had a lot of history. And just like fourteen years ago, he offered unconditional acceptance now.

His mentor leaned forward on one elbow. "What does your family have to say about all of this?"

"I've only spoken with my middle brother." He pinched off a piece of a churro drizzled with warm honey. Popping it into his mouth, he chewed and tried not think of how much of his past stayed imprinted on him.

"According to the papers, that would be Duarte. Right?" When Tony nodded, Vernon continued, "Any idea how the story broke after so many years?"

And wasn't that the million-dollar question? He, his brothers and their lawyers were no closer to the answer on that one today than they'd been last night. "Duarte doesn't have any answers yet, other than some photojournalist caught him in a snapshot and managed to track down details. Which is damn strange. None of us look the same since we left San Rinaldo as kids."

"And there are no other pictures of you in the interim?"

"Only a few stray shots after I became Tony. Carlos's face has shown up in a couple of professional magazines." But the image was so posed and sterile, Tony wasn't sure he would recognize his own sibling on the street. For the best.

His father always insisted photos would provide dangerous links, as if he'd been preparing them from the beginning to split up. Or preparing them for his death.

Not the normal way for a kid to live, but they weren't a regular family. He'd grown accustomed to it eventually... until it almost seemed normal. Until he was faced with a regular person's life, like Shannon's treasured photos of her son.

He broke off another inch of a churro. His hand slowed halfway to his mouth as he got that feeling of "being watched." He checked right fast—

Kolby stood in the open doorway, blanket trailing from his fist.

Uh, okay. So now what? He'd only met the child a few times before last night and none had gone particularly well. Tony had chalked it up to Kolby being shy around strangers or clingy. Judging by the thrust of his little jaw and frown now, there was no mistaking it. The boy didn't like him.

That needed to change. "Hey, kiddo. Where's your mom?"

Kolby didn't budge. "Still sleepin'."

Breaking the ice, Vernon tugged out a chair. "Wanna have a seat and join us?"

Never taking his eyes off Tony, Kolby padded across the tile patio and scrambled up to sit on his knees. Silently, he simply blinked and stared with wide blue-gray eyes just like Shannon's, his blond hair spiking every which way.

Vernon wiped his mouth, tossed his linen napkin on the plate and stood. "Thanks for the chow. I need to check on business. No need to see me out."

As his old friend deserted ship, unease crawled around inside Tony's gut. His experience with children was nonexistent, even when he'd been a kid himself. He and his brothers had been tutored on the island. They'd been each other's only playmates.

The island fortress had been staffed with security guards, not the mall cop sort, but more like a small deployed military unit. Cleaning staff, tutors, the chef and groundskeepers were all from San Rinaldo, older supporters of his father who'd lost their families in the coup. They shared a firm bond of loyalty, and a deep-seated need for a safe haven.

Working on the shrimp boat had felt like a vacation, with the wide open spaces and no boundaries. Most of all he enjoyed the people who didn't wear the imprint of painful loss in their eyes.

But still, there weren't any three-year-olds on the shrimp boat.

What did kids need? "Are you hungry?"

"Some of that." Kolby pointed to Tony's plate of churros. "With peanut bubber."

Grateful for action instead of awkward silence, he shoved to his feet. "Peanut butter it is then. Follow me."

Once he figured out where to look. He'd quit cooking for himself about ten years ago and the few years he had, he wasn't whipping up kiddie cuisine.

About seven minutes later he unearthed a jar from the cavernous pantry and smeared a messy trail down a churro before chunking the spoon in the sink.

Kolby pointed to the lid on the granite countertop. "We don't waste."

"Right." Tony twisted the lid on tight. Thinking of Shannon pinching pennies on peanut butter, for crying out loud, he wanted to buy them a lifetime supply.

As he started to pass the plate to Kolby, a stray thought broadsided him. Hell. Was the kid allergic to peanuts? He hadn't even thought to ask. Kolby reached. Tony swallowed another curse.

"Let's wait for your mom."

"Wait for me why?" Her softly melodic voice drifted over his shoulder from across the kitchen.

He glanced back and his heart kicked against his ribs. They'd slept together over the past month but never actually *slept*. And never through the night.

Damn, she made jeans look good, the washed pale fabric clinging to her long legs. Her hair flowed over her shoulders and down her back, still damp from a shower. He remembered well the silky glide of it through his fingers… and so not something he should be thinking about with her son watching.

Tony held up the plate of churros. "Can he eat peanut butter?"

"He's never tried it that way before, but I'm sure he'll like it." She slipped the dish from his grip. "Although, I'm not so certain that breakable stoneware is the best choice for a three-year-old."

"Hey, kiddo, is the plate all right with you?"

"'S okay." Kolby inched toward his mother and wrapped an arm around her leg. "Like trains better. And milk."

"The milk I can handle." He yanked open the door on the stainless steel refrigerator and reached for the jug. "I'll make sure you have the best train plates next time."

"Wait!" Shannon stopped him, digging into an oversized bag on her shoulder and pulling out a cup with a vented lid. "Here's his sippy cup. It's not Waterford, but it works better."

Smoothly, she filled it halfway and scooped up the plate. Kolby held on to his mother all the way back to the patio.

For the first time he wondered why he hadn't spent more time with the boy. Shannon hadn't offered and he hadn't pushed. She sat and pulled Kolby in her lap, plate in front just out of his reach. The whole family breakfast scenario wrapped around him, threatening his focus. He skimmed a finger along his shirt collar— Hell. He stopped short, realizing he wasn't wearing a tie.

She pinched off a bite and passed it to her son. "I had a lot of time to think last night."

So she hadn't slept any better than he had. "What did you think about after I left?"

Her eyes shot up to his, pink flushing her face. "Going to see your father, of course."

"Of course." He nodded, smiling.

"Of course," Kolby echoed.

As the boy licked the peanut butter off the churro, she traced the intricate pattern painted along the edge of the plate, frowning. "I would like to tell Vernon and your lawyer about our plans for the week and then I'll come with you."

He'd won. She would be safe, and he would have more time to sway her. Except it really chapped his hide that she trusted him so little she felt the need to log her travel itinerary. "Not meaning to shoot myself in the foot here, but why Vernon instead of my lawyer? Vernon is my friend. I financed his business."

"You own the restaurant?" Her slim fingers gravitated back to the china. "*You* are responsible for my paychecks? I thought the Grille belonged to Vernon."

"You didn't know?" Probably a good thing or he might well have never talked her into that first date. "Vernon was a friend when I needed one. I'm glad I could return the favor. He's more than delivered on the investment."

"He gave you a job when your past must have seemed spotty," she said intuitively.

"How did you figure that out?"

"He did the same for me when I needed a chance." A bittersweet smile flickered across her face much like how the sunlight filtered through the lemon tree to play in her hair. "That's the reason I trust him."

"You've worked hard for every penny you make there."

"I know, but I appreciate that he was fair. No handouts, and yet he never took advantage of how much I needed that job. He's a good man. Now back to our travel plans." She rested her chin on her son's head. "Just to be sure, I'll also be informing my in-laws—Kolby's grandparents."

His brows slammed upward. She rarely mentioned them, only that they'd cut her out of their lives after their son died. The fact that she would keep such cold fish informed about their grandson spoke of an innate sense of fair play he wasn't sure he would have given in her position.

"Apparently you trust just about everyone more than me."

She dabbed at the corners of her mouth, drawing his attention to the plump curve of her bottom lip. "Apparently so."

Not a ringing endorsement of her faith in him, but he would take the victory and focus forward. Because before sundown, he would return to his father's island home off the coast of Florida.

She was actually in a private plane over...

Somewhere.

Since the window shades were closed, she had no idea whether they were close to land or water. So where were they? Once airborne, she'd felt the plane turn, but quickly lost any sense of whether they were going north or south, east or west. Although north was unlikely given he'd told her to pack for warm weather.

How far had they traveled? Tough to tell since she'd napped and she had no idea how fast this aircraft could travel. She'd been swept away into a world beyond anything she'd experienced, from the discreet impeccable service to the sleeping quarters already made up for her and Kolby on arrival. Questions about her food preferences had resulted in a five-star meal.

Shannon pressed a hand to her jittery stomach. God,

she hoped she'd made the right decision. At least her son seemed oblivious to all the turmoil around them.

The cabin steward guided Kolby toward the galley kitchen with the promise of a snack and a video. As they walked toward the back, he dragged his tiny fingers along the white leather seats. At least his hands were clean.

But she would have to make a point of keeping sharp objects out of Kolby's reach. She shuddered at the image of a silver taped *X* on the luxury upholstery.

Her eyes shifted to the man filling the deep seat across from her couch. Wearing gray pants and a white shirt with the sleeves rolled up, he focused intently on the laptop screen in front of him, seemingly oblivious to anyone around him.

She hated the claustrophobic feeling of needing his help, not to mention all the money hiding out entailed. Dependence made her vulnerable, something she'd sworn would never happen again. Yet here she was, entrusting her whole life to a man, a man who'd lied to her.

However, with her child's well-being at stake, she couldn't afford to say no.

More information would help settle the apprehension plucking at her nerves like heart strings. Any information, since apparently everything she knew about him outside of the bedroom was false. She hadn't even known he owned the restaurant where she worked.

Ugh.

Of course it seemed silly to worry about being branded as the type who sleeps with the boss. Having an affair with a drop-dead sexy prince trumped any other gossip. "How long has it been since you saw your father?"

Tony looked up from his laptop slowly. "I left the island when I was eighteen."

"Island?" Her hand grazed the covered window as she

envisioned water below. "I thought you left San Rinaldo as a young boy."

"We did." He closed the computer and pivoted the chair toward her, stretching his legs until his feet stopped intimately close to hers. "I was five at the time. We relocated to another island about a month after we escaped."

She scrunched her toes in her gym shoes. Her scuffed canvas was worlds away from his polished loafers and a private plane. And regardless of how hot he looked, she wouldn't be seduced by the trappings of his wealth.

Forcing her mind back on his words rather than his body, she drew her legs away from him. Was the island on the east coast or west coast? Provided Enrique Medina's compound was even near the U.S. "Your father chose an island so you and your brothers would feel at home in your new place?"

He looked at her over the white tulips centered on the cherry coffee table. "My father chose an island because it was easier to secure."

Gulp. "Oh. Right."

That took the temperature down more than a few degrees. She picked at the piping on the sofa.

Music drifted from the back of the plane, the sound of a new cartoon starting. She glanced down the walkway. Kolby was buckled into a seat, munching on some kind of crackers while watching the movie, mesmerized. Most likely by the whopping big flat screen.

Back to her questions. "How much of you is real and what's a part of the new identity?"

"My age and birthday are real." He tucked the laptop into an oversized briefcase monogrammed with the Castillo Shipping Corporation logo. "Even my name is technically correct, as I told you before. Castillo comes from my mother's family tree. I took it as my own when I turned eighteen."

Resting her elbow on the back of the sofa, she propped her head in her palm, trying her darnedest to act as casual as he appeared. "What does your father think of all you've accomplished since leaving?"

"I wouldn't know." He reclined, folding his hands over his stomach, drawing her eyes and memories to his rock-hard abs.

Her toes curled again until they cracked inside her canvas sneakers. "What does he think of us coming now?"

"You'll have to ask him." His jaw flexed.

"Did you even tell him about the extra guests?" She resisted the urge to smooth the strain away from the bunched tendons in his neck. How odd to think of comforting him when she still had so many reservations about the trip herself.

"I told his lawyer to inform him. His staff will make preparations. Kolby will have whatever he needs."

Who was this coolly factual man a hand stretch away? She almost wondered if she'd imagined carefree Tony... except he'd told her that he liked to surf. She clung to that everyday image and dug deeper.

"Sounds like you and your father aren't close. Or is that just the way royalty communicates?" If so, how sad was that?

He didn't answer, the drone of the engines mingling with the cartoon and the rush of recycled air through the vents. While she wanted her son to grow up independent with a life of his own, she also planned to forge a bond closer than cold communications exchanged between lawyers and assistants.

"Tony?"

His eyes shifted to the shuttered window beside her

head. "I didn't want to live on a secluded island any longer. So I left. He disagreed. We haven't resolved the issue."

Such simple words for so deep a breach where attorneys handled *all* communiqués between them. The lack of communication went beyond distant to estrangement. This wasn't a family just fractured by location. Something far deeper was wrong.

Tucking back into his line of sight, she pressed ahead. This man had already left such a deep imprint on her life, she knew she wouldn't forget him. "What have your lawyers told your father about Kolby and me? What did they tell your dad about our relationship?"

"Relationship?" He pinned her with his dark eyes, the intensity of his look—of him—reaching past the tulips as tangibly as if he'd taken that broad hand and caressed her. He was such a big man with the gentlest of touches.

And he was thorough. God, how he was thorough.

Her heart pounded in her ear like a tympani solo, hollow and so loud it drowned out the engines.

"Tony?" she asked. She *wanted*.

"I let him know that we're a couple. And that you're a widow with a son."

It was one thing to carry on a secret affair with him. Another to openly acknowledge to people—to family—that they were a couple.

She pressed hard against her collarbone, her pulse pushing a syncopated beat against her fingertips. "Why not tell your father the truth? That we broke up but the press won't believe it."

"Who says it's not the truth? We slept together just a week ago. Seems like less than that to me, because I swear I can still catch a whiff of your scent on my skin." He leaned closer and thumbed her wrist.

Her fingers curled as the heat of his touch spread farther. "But about last weekend—"

"Shanny." He tapped her lips once, then traced her rounded sigh. "We may have argued, but when I'm in the room with you, my hand still gravitates to your back by instinct."

Her heart drummed faster until she couldn't have responded even if she tried. But she wasn't trying, too caught up in the sound of him, the desire in his every word.

"The pull between us is that strong, Shannon, whether I'm deep inside you or just listening to you across a room." A half smile kicked a dimple into one cheek. "Why do you think I call you late at night?"

She glanced quickly at the video area checking to make sure her son and the steward where still engrossed in Disney, then she whispered, "Because you'd finished work?"

"You know better. Just the sound of you on the other end of the line sends me rock—"

"Stop, please." She pressed her fingers to his mouth. "You're only hurting us both."

Nipping her fingers lightly first, he linked his hand with hers. "We have problems, without a doubt, and you have reason to be mad. But the drive to be together hasn't eased one bit. Can you deny it? Because if you can, then that is it. I'll keep my distance."

Opening her mouth, she formed the words that would slice that last tie to the relationship they'd forged over the past few months. She fully intended to tell him they were through…. But nothing came out. Not one word.

Slowly, he pulled back. "We're almost there."

Almost where? Back together? Her mind scrambled to keep up with him, damn tough when he kept jumbling her brain. She was a flipping magna cum laude graduate. She resented feeling like a bimbo at the mercy of her libido. But how her libido sang arias around this man…

He shoved to his feet and walked away. Just like that, he cut their conversation short as if they both hadn't been sinking deep into a sensual awareness that had brought them both such intense pleasure in the past. She tracked the lines of his broad shoulders, down to his trim waist and taut butt showcased so perfectly in tailored pants.

Her fingers dug deep into the sofa with restraint. He stopped by Kolby and slid up the window covering.

"Take a look, kiddo, we're almost there." Tony pointed at the clear glass toward the pristine sky.

Ah. *There.* As in they'd arrived there, at his father's island. She'd been so caught up in the sensual draw of undiluted Tony that she'd temporarily forgotten about flying away to a mystery location.

Scrambling down the sofa, she straightened her glasses and stared out the window, hungry for a peek at their future—temporary—home. And yes, curious as hell about the place where Tony had grown up. Sure enough, an island stretched in the distance, nestled in miles and miles of sparkling ocean. Palm trees spiked from the lush landscape. A dozen or so small outbuildings dotted a semicircle around a larger structure.

The white mansion faced the ocean in a *U* shape, constructed around a large courtyard with a pool. She barely registered Kolby's "oohs" and "aahs" since she was pretty much overwhelmed by the sight herself.

Details were spotty but she would get an up-close view soon enough of the place Tony had called home for most of his youth. Even from a distance she couldn't miss the grand scale of the sprawling estate, the unmistakable sort that housed royalty.

The plane banked, lining up with a thin islet alongside the larger island. A single strip of concrete marked the private runway. As they neared, a ferryboat came into focus. To ride from the airport to the main island? They sure were serious about security.

The intercom system crackled a second before the steward announced, "We're about to begin our descent to our destination. Please return to your seats and secure your lap belts. Thank you, and we hope you had a pleasant flight."

Tony pulled away from the window and smiled at her again. Except now, the grin didn't reach his eyes. Her stomach fluttered, but this time with apprehension rather than arousal.

Would the island hold the answers she needed to put Tony in her past? Or would it only break her heart all over again?

Five

Daylight was fading fast and a silence fourteen years old between him and his father was about to be broken.

Feet braced on the ferry deck, Tony stared out over the rail at the island where he'd spent the bulk of his childhood and teenage years. He hated not being in command of the boat almost as much as he hated returning to this place. Only concern for Shannon and her son could have drawn him back where the memories grew and spread as tenaciously as algae webbing around coral.

Just ahead, a black skimmer glided across the water, dipping its bill into the surface. With each lap of the waves against the hull, Tony closed off insidious emotions before they could take root inside him and focused on the shore.

An osprey circled over its nest. Palm trees lined the beach with only a small white stucco building and a two-lane road. Until you looked closer and saw the guard tower.

When he'd come to this island off the coast of St. Augustine at five, there were times he'd believed they were home…that his father had moved them to another part of San Rinaldo. In the darkest nights, he'd woken in a cold sweat, certain the soldiers in camouflage were going to cut through the bars on his windows and take him. Other nights he imagined they'd already taken him and the bars locked him in prison.

On the worst of nights, he'd thought his mother was still alive, only to see her die all over again.

Shannon's hand slid over his elbow, her touch tentative, her eyes wary. "How long did I sleep on the plane?"

"A while." He smiled to reassure her, but the feeling didn't come from his gut. Damn, but he wished the past week had never happened. He would pull her soft body against him and forget about everything else.

Wind streaked her hair across her face. "Oh, right. If you tell me, I might get a sense of how far away we are from Galveston. I might guess where we are. Being cut off from the world is still freaking me out just a little."

"I understand, and I'll to do my best to set things right as soon as possible." He wanted nothing more than to get off this island and return to the life he'd built, the life he chose. The only thing that made coming back here palatable was having Shannon by his side. And that rocked the deck under his feet, realizing she held so much influence over his life.

"Although, I have to admit," she conceded as she tucked her son closer, "this place is so much more than I expected."

Her gaze seemed to track the herons picking their way along the shore, sea oats bowing at every gust. Her grayish-blue eyes glinted with the first hints of excitement. She must not have noticed the security cameras tucked in trees and the guard on the dock, a gun strapped within easy reach.

Tony gripped the rail tighter. "There's no way to prepare a person."

Kolby squealed, pitching forward in his mother's arms.

"Whoa..." Tony snagged the kid by the back of his striped overalls. "Steady there."

A hand pressed to her chest, Shannon struggled for breath. "Thank God you moved so fast. I can't believe I looked away. There's just so much to see, so many distractions."

The little guy scowled at Tony. "Down."

"Buddy," Tony stated as he shook his head, "sometime you're going to have to like me."

"Name's not buddy," Kolby insisted, bottom lip out.

"You're right. I'm just trying to make friends here." Because he intended to use this time to persuade Shannon breaking up had been a crappy idea. He wondered how much the child understood. Since he didn't know how else to approach him, he opted for straight up honesty. "I like your mom, so it's important that you like me."

Shannon's gasp teased his ear like a fresh trickle of wind off the water. As much as he wanted to turn toward her, he kept his attention on the boy.

Kolby clenched Tony's shirt. "Does you like *me?*"

"Uh, sure." The question caught him off guard. He hadn't thought about it other than knowing it was important to win the son over for Shannon's sake. "What do you like?"

"Not you." He popped his bottom lip back in. "Down, pwease."

Shannon caught her son as he leaned toward her. Confusion puckering her brow, her eyes held Tony's for a second before she pointed over the side. "Is that what you wanted to see, sweetie?"

A dolphin zipped alongside the ferry. The fin sliced through the water, then submerged again.

Clapping his tiny hands, Kolby chanted, "Yes, yes, yes."

Again, Shannon saw beauty. He saw something entirely different. The dolphins provided port security. His father had gotten the idea from his own military service, cutting-edge stuff back then. The island was a minikingdom and money wasn't an object. Except this kingdom had substantially fewer subjects.

Tony wondered again if the secluded surroundings growing up could have played into his lousy track record with relationships as an adult. There hadn't been any teenage dating rituals for practice. And after he left, he'd been careful with relationships, never letting anything get too complicated. Work and a full social life kept him happy.

But the child in front of him made things problematic in a way he hadn't foreseen.

For years he'd been pissed off at his father for the way they'd had to live. And here he was doing the same to Kolby. The kid was entertained for the moment, but that would end fast for sure.

Protectiveness for both the mother and son seared his veins. He wouldn't let anything from the Medina past mark their future. Even if that meant he had to reclaim the very identity he'd worked his entire adulthood to shed.

The ferry slid against the dock. They'd arrived at the island.

And Prince Antonio Medina was back.

What was it like for Tony to come back after so long away? And it wasn't some happy homecoming, given the estrangement and distance in this family that communicated through lawyers.

Shannon wanted to reach across the limousine to him, but Tony had emotionally checked out the moment the ferry docked. Of course he'd been Mr. Manners while leaving the ferry and stepping into the Mercedes limo.

Watch your step... Need help? However, the smiles grew darker by the minute.

Maybe it was her own gloomy thoughts tainting her perceptions. At least Kolby seemed unaffected by their moods, keeping his nose pressed to the window the whole winding way to the pristine mansion.

Who wouldn't stare at the trees and the wildlife and finally, the palatial residence? White stucco with a clay tiled roof, arches and opulence ten times over, the place was the size of some hotels or convention centers. Except no hotel she'd stayed in sported guards armed with machine guns.

What should have made her feel safer only served to remind her money and power didn't come without burdens. To think, Tony had grown up with little or no exposure to the real world. It was a miracle he'd turned out normal.

If you could call a billionaire prince with a penchant for surfing "normal."

The limousine slowed, easing past a towering marble fountain with a "welcome" pineapple on top—and wasn't that ironic in light of all those guards? Once the vehicle stopped, more uniformed security appeared from out of nowhere to open the limo. Some kind of servant—a butler perhaps—stood at the top of the stairs. While Tony had insisted he wanted nothing to do with his birthplace, he seemed completely at ease in this surreal world. For the first time, the truth really sunk in.

The stunningly handsome—stoically silent—man walking beside her had royal blood singing through his veins.

"Tony?" She touched his elbow.

"After you," he said, simply gesturing ahead to the double doors sweeping open.

Scooping Kolby onto her hip, she took comfort in his sturdy little body and forged ahead. Inside. *Whoa*.

The cavernous circular hall sported gold gilded archways leading to open rooms. Two staircases stretched up either side, meeting in the middle. And, uh, stop the world, was that a Picasso on the wall?

Her canvas sneakers squeaked against marble floors as more arches ushered her deeper into the mansion. And while she vowed money didn't matter, she still wished she'd packed different shoes. Shannon straightened the straps on Kolby's favorite striped overalls, the ones he swore choo-choo drivers wore. She'd been so frazzled when she'd tossed clothes into a couple of overnight bags, picking things that would make him happy.

Just ahead, French doors opened on to a veranda that overlooked the ocean. Tony turned at the last minute, guiding her toward what appeared to be a library. Books filled three walls, interspersed with windows and a sliding brass ladder. Mosaic tiles swirled outward on the floor, the ceiling filled with frescos of globes and conquistadors. The smell of fresh citrus hung in the air, and not just because of the open windows. A tall potted orange tree nestled in one corner beneath a wide skylight.

An older man slept in a wingback by the dormant fireplace. Two large brown dogs—some kind of Ridgeback breed, perhaps?—lounged to his left and right.

Tony's father. A no-kidding king.

Either age or illness had taken a toll, dimming the family resemblance. But in spite of his nap, he wasn't going gently into that good night. No slippers and robe for this meeting. He wore a simple black suit with an ascot rather than a tie, his silver hair slicked back. Frailty and his pasty pallor made her want to comfort him.

Then his eyes snapped open. The sharp gleam in his coal dark eyes stopped her short.

Holy Sean Connery, the guy might be old but he hadn't lost his edge.

"Welcome home, *hijo prodigo*." *Prodigal son*.

Enrique Medina spoke in English but his accent was still unmistakably Spanish. And perhaps a bit thick with emotion? Or was that just wishful thinking on her part for Tony's sake?

"Hello, Papa." Tony palmed her back between her shoulder blades. "This is Shannon and her son Kolby."

The aging monarch nodded in her direction. "Welcome, to you and to your son."

"Thank you for your hospitality and your help, sir." She didn't dare wade into the whole *Your Highness* versus *Your Majesty* waters. Simplicity seemed safest.

Toying with a pocket watch in his hand, Enrique continued, "If not for my family, you would not need my assistance."

Tony's fingers twitched against her back. "Hopefully we won't have to impose upon you for long. Shannon and her son only need a place to lay low until this blows over."

"It won't blow over," Enrique said simply.

Ouch. She winced.

Tony didn't. "Poor choice of words. Until things calm down."

"Of course." He nodded regally before shifting his attention her way. "I am glad to have you here, my dear. You brought Tony home, so you have already won favor with me." He smiled and for the first time, she saw the family resemblance clearly.

Kolby wriggled, peeking up from her neck. "Whatsa matter with you?"

"Shhh...Kolby." She pressed a quick silencing kiss to his forehead. "That's a rude question."

"It's an honest question. I do not mind the boy." The king shifted his attention to her son. "I have been ill. My legs are not strong enough to walk."

"I'm sorry." Kolby eyed the wheelchair folded up and tucked discreetly alongside the fireplace. "You musta been bery sick."

"Thank you. I have good doctors."

"You got germs?"

A smile tugged at the stern face. "No, child. You and your mother cannot catch my germs."

"That's good." He stuffed his tiny fists into his pockets. "Don't like washin' my hands."

Enrique laughed low before his hand fell to rest on one dog's head. "Do you like animals?"

"Yep." Kolby squirmed downward until Shannon had no choice but to release him before he pitched out of her arms. "Want a dog."

Such a simple, painfully normal wish and she couldn't afford to supply it. From the pet deposit required at her apartment complex to the vet bills... It was out of her budget. Guilt tweaked again over all she couldn't give her child.

Yet hadn't Tony been denied so much even with such wealth? He'd lost his home, his mother and gained a gilded prison. Whispers of sympathy for a motherless boy growing up isolated from the world softened her heart when she most needed to hold strong.

Enrique motioned Kolby closer. "You may pet my dog.

Come closer and I will introduce you to Benito and Diablo. They are very well trained and will not hurt you."

Kolby didn't even hesitate. Any reservations her son felt about Tony certainly didn't extend to King Enrique—or his dogs. Diablo sniffed the tiny, extended hand.

A cleared throat startled Shannon from her thoughts. She glanced over her shoulder and found a young woman waiting in the archway. In her late twenties, wearing a Chanel suit, she obviously wasn't the housekeeper.

But she was stunning with her black hair sleeked back in a simple clasp. She wore strappy heels instead of sneakers. God, it felt silly to be envious of someone she didn't know, and honestly, she only coveted the pretty red shoes.

"Alys," the older man commanded, "enter. Come meet my son and his guests. This is my assistant, Alys Reyes de la Cortez. She will show you to your quarters."

Shannon resisted the urge to jump to conclusions. It wasn't any of her business who Enrique Medina chose for his staff and she shouldn't judge a person by their appearance. The woman was probably a rocket scientist, and Shannon wouldn't trade one single sticky hug from her son for all the high-end clothes on the planet.

Not that she was jealous of the gorgeous female with immaculate clothes, who fit perfectly into Tony's world. After all, he hadn't spared more than a passing glance at the woman.

Still, she wished she'd packed a pair of pumps.

An hour later, Shannon closed her empty suitcases and rocked back on her bare heels in the doorway of her new quarters.

A suite?

More like a luxury condominium within the mansion. She sunk her toes into the Persian rug until her chipped pink polish disappeared in the apricot and gray pattern. She and Kolby had separate bedrooms off a sitting area with an eating space stocked more fully than most kitchens. The balcony was as large as some yards.

Had the fresh-cut flowers been placed in here just for her? She dipped her face into the crystal vase of lisianthus with blooms that resembled blue roses and softened the gray tones in the decor.

After Alys had walked them up the lengthy stairs to their suite, Kolby had run from room to room for fifteen minutes before winding down and falling asleep in an exhausted heap under the covers. He hadn't even noticed the toy box at the end of his sleigh bed yet, he'd been so curious about their new digs. Tony had given them space while she unpacked, leaving for his quarters with a simple goodbye and another of those smiles that didn't reach his eyes.

The quiet echoed around her, leaving her hyperaware of other sounds…a ticking grandfather clock in the hall… the crashing ocean outside… Trailing her fingers along the camelback sofa, she looked through the double doors, moonlight casting shadows along her balcony. Her feet drew her closer until the shadows took shape into the broad shoulders of a man leaning on the railing.

Tony? He felt like a safe haven in an upside down day. But how had he gotten there without her noticing his arrival?

Their balconies must connect, which meant someone had planned for them to have access to each other's rooms. Had he been waiting for her? Anticipation hummed through her at the notion of having him all to herself.

Shannon unlocked and pushed open the doors to the patio filled with topiaries, ferns and flowering cacti. A swift ocean breeze rolled over her, lifting her hair and fluttering her shirt along her skin in whispery caresses. God, she was tired and emotional and so not in the right frame of mind to be anywhere near Tony. She should go to bed instead of staring at his sinfully sexy body just calling to her to rest her cheek on his back and wrap her arms around his waist. Her fingers fanned against her legs as she remembered the feel of him, so much more intense with his sandalwood scent riding the wind.

Need pooled warm and languid and low, diluting her already fading resistance.

His shoulders bunched under his starched white shirt a second before he glanced over his shoulder, his eyes haunted. Then they cleared. "Is Kolby asleep?"

"Yes, and thank you for all the preparations. The toys, the food…the flowers."

"All a part of the Medina welcome package."

"Perhaps." But she'd noticed a few too many of their favorites for the choices to have been coincidental. She moved forward hesitantly, the tiles cool against the bottoms of her feet. "This is all…something else."

"Leaving San Rinaldo, we had to downsize." He gave her another of those dry smiles.

More sympathy slid over her frustration at his secrets. "Thank you for bringing us here. I know it wasn't easy for you."

"I'm the reason you have to hide out in the first place until we line up protection for you. Seems only fair I should do everything in my power to make this right."

Her husband had never tried to fix any of his mistakes, hadn't even apologized after his arrest in the face of irrefutable evidence. She couldn't help but appreciate the way Tony took responsibility. And he cared enough to smooth the way for her.

"What about you?" She joined him at the swirled iron

railing. "You wouldn't have come here if it weren't for me. What do you hope to accomplish for yourself?"

"Don't worry about me." He leaned back on his elbows, white shirt stretching open at the collar to reveal the strong column of his neck. "I always look out for myself."

"Then what are you gaining?"

"More time with you, at least until the restraining order is in place." The heat of his eyes broadcast his intent just before he reached for her. "I've always been clear about how much I want to be with you, even on that first date when you wouldn't kiss me good-night."

"Is that why you chased me? Because I said no?"

"But you didn't keep saying no and still, here I am turned on as hell by the sound of your voice." He plucked her glasses off, set them aside and cradled her face in his palms. "The feel of your skin."

While he owned an empire with corporate offices that took up a bayside block, his skin still carried the calluses of the dockworker and sailor he'd been during his early adulthood. He was a man who certainly knew how to work with his hands. The rasp as he lightly caressed her cheekbones reminded her of the sweet abrasion when he explored farther.

He combed through along her scalp, strands slithering across his fingers. "The feel of your hair."

A moan slipped past her lips along with his name, "Tony…"

"Antonio," he reminded her. "I want to hear you say my name, know who's here with you."

And in this moment, in his eyes, he was that foreign prince, less accessible than her Tony, but no less exciting and infinitely as irresistible, so she whispered, "Antonio."

His touch was gentle, his mouth firm against hers. She parted her lips under his and invited in the familiar sweep, taste and pure sensation. Clutching his elbows, she swayed, her breasts tingling, pulling tight. Before she could think or stop herself, she brushed slightly from side to side, increasing the sweet pleasure of his hard chest teasing her. His hard thigh between her legs.

She stepped backward.

And tugged him with her.

Toward the open French doors leading into her bedroom, her body overriding her brain as it always seemed to do around Tony. She squeezed her legs together tighter against the firm pressure of his muscled thigh, so close, too close. She wanted, *needed* to feel him move inside her first.

Sinking her fingernails deeper, she ached to ask him to stay with her, to help her forget the worries waiting at home. "Antonio—"

"I know." He eased his mouth from hers, his chin scraping along her jaw as he nuzzled her hair and inhaled. "We need to stop."

Stop? She almost shrieked in frustration. "But I thought... I mean, you're here and usually when we let things go this far, we finish."

"You're ready to resume our affair?"

Affair. Not just one night, one satisfaction, but a relationship with implications and complications. Her brain raced to catch up after being put on idle while her body took over. God, what had she almost done? A few kisses along with a well-placed thigh, and she was ready to throw herself back in his bed.

Planting her hands on his chest, she stepped away. "I can't deny that I miss you and I want you, but I have no desire to be labeled a Medina mistress."

His eyebrows shot up toward his hairline. "Are you saying you want to get married?"

Six

"Married?" Shannon choked on the word, her eyes so wide with shock Tony was almost insulted. "No! No, definitely not."

Her instant and emphatic denial left zero room for doubt. She wasn't expecting a proposal. Good thing, since that hadn't crossed his mind. Until now.

Was he willing to go that far to protect her?

She turned away fast, her hands raised as she raced back into the sitting area. "Tony—Antonio—I can't talk to you, look at you, risk kissing you again. I need to go to bed. To sleep. Alone."

"Then what do you want from me?"

"To end this craziness. To stop thinking about you all the time."

All the time?

He homed in on her words, an obvious slip on her part because while she'd been receptive and enthusiastic in bed, she'd given him precious little encouragement once they had their clothes back on again. Their fight over his simple offer of money still stung. Why did she have to reject his attempt to help?

She paced, restlessly lining up her shoes beside the sofa, scooping Kolby's tiny train from a table, lingering to rearrange the blue flowers. "You've said you feel the same. Who the hell wants to be consumed by this kind of ache all the time? It's damned inconvenient, especially when it can't lead anywhere. It's not like you were looking for marriage."

"That wasn't my intention when we started seeing each other." Yet somehow the thought had popped into his head out there on the patio. Sure, it had shocked the crap out of him at first. Still left him reeling. Although not so much that he was willing to reject the idea outright. "But since you've brought it up—"

Her hands shot up in front of her, between them. "Uh-uh, no sirree. You were the one to mention the *M* word."

"Fine, then. The marriage issue is out there, on the table for discussion. Let's talk it through."

She stopped cold. "This isn't some kind of business merger. We're talking about our lives here, and not just ours. I don't have the luxury of making another mistake. I already screwed up once before, big time. My son's well-being depends on my decisions."

"And I'm a bad choice because?"

"Do not play with my feelings. Damn it, Tony." She jabbed him in the chest with one finger. "You know I'm attracted to you. If you keep this up, I'll probably cave and we'll have sex. We probably would have on the plane if the steward and my son hadn't been around. But I would have been sorry the minute the orgasm chilled and is that really how you want it to be between us? To have me waking up regretting it every time?"

With images of the two of them joining the mile-high club fast-tracking from his brain to his groin, he seriously considered saying to hell with regrets. Let this insanity between them play out, wherever it took them.

Her bed was only a few steps away, offering a clear and tempting place to sink inside her. He would sweep away her clothes and the covers— His gaze hooked on the afghan draped along the end corner of the mattress.

Damn. Who had put that there? Could his father be deliberately jabbing him with reminders of their life as a family in hopes of drawing him back into the fold? Of course Enrique would, manipulative old cuss that he was.

That familiar silver blanket sucker punched him back to reality. He would recognize the one-of-a-kind afghan anywhere. His mother had knitted it for him just before she'd been killed, and he'd kept it with him like a shield during the whole hellish escape from San Rinaldo. Good God, he shouldn't have had to ask her why he was a bad choice. He knew the reason well.

Tony stumbled back, away from the memories and away from this woman who saw too much with her perceptive gray-blue eyes.

"You're right, Shannon. We're both too exhausted to make any more decisions today. Sleep well." His voice as raw as his memory-riddled gut, he left.

Dazed, Shannon stood in the middle of the sitting room wondering what the hell had just happened.

One second she'd been ready to climb back into Tony's arms and bed, the next they'd been talking about marriage.

And didn't that still stun her numb with thoughts of how horribly things had ended with Nolan?

But only seconds after bringing up the marriage issue, Tony had emotionally checked out on her again. At least he'd prevented them from making a mistake. It was a mistake, right?

Eyeing her big—empty—four-poster bed, she suddenly wasn't one bit sleepy. Tony overwhelmed her as much as the wealth. She walked into her bedroom, studying the Picasso over her headboard, this one from the artist's rose period, a harlequin clown in oranges and pinks. She'd counted three works already by this artist alone, including some leggy elephant painting in Kolby's room.

She'd hidden the crayons and markers.

Laughing at the absurdity of it all, she fingered a folded cashmere afghan draped over the corner of the mattress. So whispery soft and strangely worn in the middle of this immaculately opulent decor. The pewter-colored yarn complemented the apricot and gray tones well enough, but she wondered where it had come from. She tugged it from the bed and shook it out.

The blanket rippled in front of her, a little larger than a lap quilt, not quite long enough for a single bed. Turning in a circle she wrapped the filmy cover around her and padded back out to the balcony. She hugged the cashmere wrap tighter and curled up in a padded lounger, letting the ocean wind soothe her face still warm from Tony's touch.

Was it her imagination or could she smell hints of him even on the blanket? Or was he that firmly in her senses as well as her thoughts? What was it about Tony that reached to her in ways Nolan never had? She'd responded to her husband's touch, found completion, content with her life right up to the point of betrayal.

But Tony... Shannon hugged the blanket tighter. She

hadn't been hinting at marriage, damn it. Just the thought of giving over her life so completely again scared her to her toes.

So where did that leave her? Seriously considering becoming exactly what the media labeled her—a monarch's mistress.

Tony heard...the silence.

Finally, Shannon had settled for the night. Thank God. Much longer and his willpower would have given out. He would have gone back into her room and picked up where they'd left off before he'd caught sight of the damn blanket.

This place screwed with his head, so much so he'd actually brought up marriage, for crying out loud. It was like there were rogue waves from his past curling up everywhere and knocking him off balance. The sooner he could take care of business with his father the sooner he could return to Galveston with Shannon, back to familiar ground where he stood a better chance at reconciling with her.

Staying out of her bed for now was definitely the wiser choice. He walked down the corridor, away from her and that blanket full of memories. He needed his focus sharp for the upcoming meeting with his father. This time, he would face the old man alone.

Charging down the hall, he barely registered the familiar antique wooden benches tucked here, a strategic table and guard posted there. Odd how quickly he slid right back into the surroundings even after so long away. And even stranger that his father hadn't changed a thing.

The day had been one helluva ride, and it wasn't over yet. Enrique had been with his nurse for the past hour, but should be ready to receive him now.

Tony rounded the corner and nodded to the sentinel outside the open door to Enrique's personal quarters. The space was made for a man, no feminine touches to soften the room full of browns and tans, leather and wood. Enrique saved his Salvador Dali collection for himself, a trio of the surrealist's "soft watches" melting over landscapes.

The old guy had become more obsessed with history after his had been stolen from him.

Enrique waited in his wheelchair, wearing a heavy blue robe and years of worries.

"Sit," his father ordered, pointing to his old favored chair.

When Tony didn't jump at his command, Enrique sighed heavily and muttered under his breath in Spanish. "Have a seat," he continued in his native tongue. "We need to talk, *mi hijo.*"

They did, and Tony had to admit he was curious— concerned—about his father's health. Knowing might not have brought him home sooner, but now that he was here, he couldn't ignore the gaunt angles and sallow pallor. "How sick are you really?" Tony continued in Spanish, having spoken both languages equally once they'd left San Rinaldo. "No sugar coating it. I deserve the truth."

"And you would have heard it earlier if you had returned when I first requested."

His father had never *requested* anything in his life. The stubborn old cuss had been willing to die alone rather than actually admit how ill he was.

Of course Antonio had been just as stubborn about ignoring the demands to show his face on the island. "I am here now."

"You and your brothers have stirred up trouble." A great big *I told you so* was packed into that statement.

"Do you have insights as to how this leaked? How did

that reporter identify Duarte?" His middle brother wasn't exactly a social guy.

"Nobody knows, but my people are still looking into it. I thought you would be the one to expose us," his father said wryly. "You always were the impetuous one. Yet you've behaved decisively and wisely. You have protected those close to you. Well done."

"I am past needing your approval, but I thank you for your help."

"Fair enough, and I'm well aware that you would not have accepted that help if Shannon Crawford was not involved. I would be glad to see one of my sons settled and married before I die."

His gut pitched much like a boat tossed by a wave. "Your illness is that bad?" An uneasy silence settled, his father's rattling breaths growing louder and louder. "Should I call a nurse?"

Or his assistant? He wasn't sure what Alys Reyes de la Cortez was doing here, but she was definitely different from the older staff of San Rinaldo natives Enrique normally hired.

"I may be old and sick, but I don't need to be tucked into bed like a child." His chin tipped.

"I'm not here to fight with you."

"Of course not. You're here for my help."

And he had the feeling his father wasn't going to let him forget it. They'd never gotten along well and apparently that hadn't changed. He started to rise. "If that's all then, I will turn in."

"Wait." His father polished his eighteen-karat gold pocket watch with his thumb. "My assistance comes at a price."

Shocked at the calculating tone, Tony sank back into his chair. "You can't be serious."

"I am. Completely."

He should have suspected and prepared himself. "What do you want?"

"I want you to stay for the month while you wait for the new safety measures to be implemented."

"Here? That's all?" He made it sound offhand but already he could feel the claustrophobia wrap around his throat and tighten. The Dali art mocked him with just how slippery time could be, a life that ended in a flash or a moment that extended forever.

"Is it so strange I want to see what kind of man you have matured into?"

Given Enrique had expected Tony to break their cover, he must not have had high expectations for his youngest son. And that pissed him off. "If I don't agree? You'll do what? Feed Shannon and her son to the lions?"

"Her son can stay. I would never sacrifice a child's safety. The mother will have to go."

He couldn't be serious. Tony studied his father for some sign Enrique was bluffing…but the old guy didn't have a "tell." And his father hadn't hesitated to trust his own wife's safety to others. What would stop him from sending Shannon off with a guard and a good-luck wish?

"She would never leave without her child." Like his mother. Tony restrained a wince.

"That is not my problem. Are you truly that unwilling to spend a month here?"

"What if the restraining order comes through sooner?"

"I would ask you to stay as a thanks for my assistance. I have risked a lot for you in granting her access to the island."

True enough, or so it would feel to Enrique with his near agoraphobic need to stay isolated from the world.

"And there are no other conditions?"

A salt and pepper eyebrow arched. "Do you want a contract?"

"Do you? If Shannon decides to leave by the weekend, I could simply go, too. What's the worst you can do? Cut me out of the will?" He hadn't taken a penny of his father's money.

"You always were the most amusing of my sons. I have missed that."

"I'm not laughing."

His father's smile faded and he tucked the watch into a pocket, chain jingling to a rest. "Your word is sufficient. You may not want any part of me and my little world here, but you are a Medina. You are my son. Your honor is not in question."

"Fair enough. If you're willing to accept my word, then a month it is." Now that the decision was made, he wondered why his father had chosen that length of time. "What's your prognosis?"

"My liver is failing," Enrique said simply without any hint of self-pity. "Because of the living conditions when I was on the run, I caught hepatitis. It has taken a toll over the years."

Thinking back, Tony tried to remember if his father had been sick when they'd reunited in South America before relocating to the island…but he only recalled his father being coolly determined. "I didn't know. I'm sorry."

"You were a child. You did not need to be informed of everything."

He hadn't been told much of *anything* in those days, but even if he had, he wasn't sure he would have heard. His grief for his mother had been deep and dark. That, he remembered well. "How much longer do you have?"

"I am not going to kick off in the next thirty days."

"That isn't what I meant."

"I know." His father smiled, creases digging deep. "I have a sense of humor, too."

What had his father been like before this place? Before the coup? Tony would never know because time was melting away like images in the Dali paintings on the wall.

While he had some memories of his mother from that time, he had almost none of his father until Enrique had met up with them in South America. The strongest memory he had of Enrique in San Rinaldo? When his father gathered his family to discuss the evacuation plan. Enrique had pressed his pocket watch into Tony's hands and promised to reclaim it. But even at five, Tony had known his father was saying goodbye for what could have been the last time. Now, Enrique wanted him back to say goodbye for the last time again.

How damned ironic. He'd brought Shannon to this place because she needed him. And now he could only think of how much he needed to be with her.

Seven

Where was Tony?

The next day after lunch, Shannon stood alone on her balcony overlooking the ocean. Seagulls swooped on the horizon while long legged blue herons stalked prey on the rocks. Kolby was napping. A pot of steeped herbal tea waited on a tiny table along with dried fruits and nuts.

How strange to have such complete panoramic peace during such a tumultuous time. The balcony offered an unending view of the sea, unlike the other side with barrier islands. The temperature felt much the same as in Galveston, humid and in the seventies.

She should make the most of the quiet to regain her footing. Instead, she kept looking at the door leading into Tony's suite and wondering why she hadn't seen him yet.

Her morning had been hectic and more than a little overwhelming learning her way around the mansion with Alys. As much as she needed to resist Tony, she'd missed having his big comforting presence at her side while she explored the never-ending rooms packed nonchalantly with priceless art and antiques.

And they'd only toured half of the home and grounds.

Afterward, Alys had introduced two women on hand for sitter and nanny duties. Shannon had been taken aback by the notion of turning her son over to total strangers, although she had to confess, the guard assigned to shadow Kolby reassured her. She'd been shown letters of recommendation and résumés for each individual. Still, Shannon had spent the rest of the morning getting to know each person in case she needed to call on their help.

Interestingly, none of the king's employees gave away the island's location despite subtle questions about traveling back to their homes. Everyone on Enrique's payroll seemed to understand the importance of discretion, as well as seeing to her every need. Including delivering a closet full of clothes that just happened to fit. Not that she'd caved to temptation yet and tried any of it on. A gust rolling off the ocean teased the well-washed cotton of her sundress around her legs as she stood on the balcony.

The click of double doors opening one suite down snapped her from her reverie. She didn't even need to look over her shoulder to verify who'd stepped outside. She knew the sound of his footsteps, recognized the scent of him on the breeze.

"Hello, Tony."

His Italian loafers stopped alongside her feet in simple pink and brown striped flip-flops. *Hers.* Not ones from the new stash.

Leaning into her line of sight, he rested his elbows on the iron rail. "Sorry not to have checked in on you sooner. My father and I spent the morning troubleshooting on a conference call with my brothers and our attorneys."

Of course. That made sense. "Any news?"

"More of the same. Hopefully we can start damage control with some valid info leaked to the press to turn the tide. There's just so much out there." He shook his head sharply then forced a smile. "Enough of that. I missed you at lunch."

"Kolby and I ate in our suite." The scent of Tony's sandalwood aftershave had her curling her toes. "His table manners aren't up to royal standards."

"You don't have to hide in your rooms. There's no court or ceremony here." Still, he wore khakis and a monogrammed blue button-down rolled up at the sleeves rather than the jeans and shorts most everyday folks would wear on a beach vacation.

And he looked mighty fine in every starched inch of fabric.

"Formality or not, there are priceless antiques and art all easily within a child's reach." She trailed her fingers along the iron balustrade. "This place is a lot to absorb. We need time. Although I hope life returns to normal sooner rather than later."

Could she simply pick up where she'd left off? Things hadn't been so great then, given her nearly bankrupt account and her fight with Tony over more than money, over her very independence. Yet hadn't she been considering resuming the affair just last night?

Sometimes it was tough to tell if her hormones or her heart had control these days.

He extended his hand. "You're right. Let's slow things down. Would you like to go for a walk?"

"But Kolby might wake up and ask for m—"

"One of the nannies can watch over him and call us the second his eyes open. Come on. I'll update you on the wackiest of the internet buzz." A half grin tipped one side of his tanned face. "Apparently one source thinks the Medinas have a space station and I've taken you to the mother ship."

Laughter bubbled, surprising her, and she just let it roll free with the wind tearing in from the shore. God, how she needed it after the stressful past couple of days—a stressful week for that matter, since she had broken off her relationship with Tony. "Lead the way, my alien lover."

His smile widened, reaching his eyes for the first time since their ferry had pulled up to the island. The power outshone the world around her until she barely noticed the opulent surroundings on their way through the mansion to the beach.

The October sun high in the sky was blinding and warm, hotter than when she'd been on the balcony, inching up toward eighty degrees perhaps. Her mind started churning with possible locations. Could they be in Mexico or South America? Or were they still in the States? California or—

"We're off the coast of Florida."

Glancing up sharply, she swallowed hard, not realizing until that moment how deeply the secrecy had weighed on her. "Thank you."

He waved aside her gratitude. "You would have figured it out on your own in a couple of days."

Maybe, but given the secrecy of Enrique's employees, she wasn't as certain. "So, what about more of those wacky internet rumors?"

"Do you really want to discuss that?"

"I guess not." She slid off her flip-flops and curled her toes in the warm sand. "Thank you for all the clothes for me and for Kolby, the toys, too. We'll enjoy them while we're here. But you know we can't keep them."

"Don't be a buzz kill." He tapped her nose just below the

bridge of her glasses. "My father's staff ordered everything. I had nothing to do with it. If it'll make you happy, we'll donate the lot to Goodwill after you leave."

"How did he get everything here so fast?" She strode into the tide, her shoes dangling from her fingers.

"Does it matter?" He slid off his shoes and socks and joined her, just into the water's reach.

With the more casual and familiar Tony returning, some of the tension left her shoulders. "I guess not. The toys are awesome, of course, but Kolby enjoys the dogs most. They seem incredibly well trained."

"They are. My father will have his trainers working with the dogs to bond with your son so they will protect him as well if need be while you are here."

She shivered in spite of the bold beams of sunshine overhead. "Can't a dog just be a pet?"

"Things aren't that simple for us." He looked away, down the coast at an osprey spreading its wings and diving downward.

How many times had he watched the birds as a child and wanted to fly away, too? She understood well the need to escape a golden cage. "I'm sorry."

"Don't be." He rejected her sympathy outright.

Pride iced his clipped words, and she searched for a safer subject.

Her eyes settled on the rippling crests of foam frosting the gray-blue shore. "Is this where you used to surf?"

"Actually, the cove is pretty calm." He pointed ahead to an outcropping packed with palm trees. "The best spot is about a mile and a half down. Or at least it was. Who knows after so many years?"

"You really had free rein to run around the island." She stepped onto a sandbar that fingered out into the water. As a mother, she had a tough time picturing her child exploring this junglelike beach at will.

"Once I was a teenager, pretty much. After I was through with schooling for the day, of course." A green turtle popped his head from the water, legs poking from the shell as he swam out and slapped up the beach. "Although sometimes we even had class out here."

"A field trip to the beach? What fun teachers you had."

"Tutors."

"Of course." The stark difference in their upbringings wrapped around her like seaweed lapping at her ankles. She tried to shake free of the clammy negativity. "Surfing was your P.E.?"

"Technically, we had what you would call phys ed, but it was more of a health class with martial arts training."

During her couple of years teaching high school band and chorus before she'd met Nolan, some of her students went to karate lessons. But they'd gone to a gym full of other students, rather than attending in seclusion with only two brothers for company. "It's so surreal to think you never went to prom, or had an after-school job or played on a basketball team."

"We had games here…but you're right in that there was no stadium of classmates and parents. No cheerleaders." He winked and smiled, but she sensed he was using levity as a diversion.

How often had he done that in the past and she'd missed out hearing his real thoughts or feelings because she wanted things to be uncomplicated?

Shannon squeezed his bulging forearm. "You would have been a good football player with your size."

"Soccer." His bicep twitched under her touch. "I'm from Europe, remember?"

"Of course." Unlikely she would ever forget his roots now that she knew. And she wanted to learn more about this strong-jawed man who thought to order a miniature motorized Jeep for her son—and then give credit to his father.

She tucked her hand into the crook of his arm as she swished through the ebbs and flow of the tidewaters. "So you still think of yourself as being from Europe? Even though you were only five when you came to the U.S.?"

His eyebrows pinched together. "I never really thought of this as the U.S. even though I know how close we are."

"I can understand that. Everything here is such a mix of cultures." While the staff spoke English to her, she'd heard Spanish spoken by some. Books and magazines and even instructions on labels were a mix of English, Spanish and some French. "You mentioned thinking this was still San Rinaldo when you got here."

"Only at first. My father told us otherwise."

What difficult conversations those must have been between father and sons. So much to learn and adjust to so young. "We've both lost a lot, you and I. I wonder if I sensed that on some level, if that's what drew us to each other."

He slid an arm around her shoulders and pulled her closer while they kicked through the surf. "Don't kid yourself. I was attracted to how hot you looked walking away in that slim black skirt. And then when you glanced over your shoulder with those prim glasses and do-me eyes." He whistled long and low. "I was toast from the get-go."

Trying not to smile, her skin heating all the same, she elbowed him lightly. "Cro-Magnon."

"Hey, I'm a red-blooded male and you're sexy." He traced the cat-eye edge of her glasses. "You're also entirely too serious at the moment. Life will kick us in the ass all on its own soon enough. We're going to just enjoy the moment, remember? No more buzz kills."

"You're right." Who knew how much longer she would have with Tony before this mess blew up in her face? "Let's go back to talking about surfing and high school dances. You so would have been the bad boy."

"And I'll bet you were a good girl. Did you wear those studious glasses even then?"

"Since I was in the eighth grade." She'd hated how her nose would sweat in the heat when she'd marched during football games. "I was a dedicated musician with no time for boys."

"And now?"

"I want to enjoy this beautiful ocean and a day with absolutely nothing to do." She bolted ahead, kicking through the tide, not sure how to balance her impulsive need for Tony with her practical side that demanded she stay on guard.

Footsteps splashed behind her a second before Tony scooped her up. And she let him.

The warm heat of his shoulder under her cheek, the steady pump of his heart against her side had her curling her arms around his neck. "You're getting us all wet."

His eyes fell to her shirt. His heart thumped faster. "Are you having fun?"

"Yes, I am." She toyed with the springy curls at the nape of his neck. "You always make sure of that, whether it's an opera or a walk by the beach."

"You deserve to have more fun in your life." He held her against his chest with a familiarity she couldn't deny. "I would make things easier for you. You know that."

"And you know where I stand on that subject." She cupped his face, his stubble so dark and thick that he wore a perpetual five o'clock shadow. "This—your protection, the trip, the clothes and toys—it's already much more than I'm comfortable taking."

She needed to be clear on that before she even considered letting him closer again.

He eased her to her feet with a lingering glide of her body down his. "We should go back."

The desire in his eyes glinted unmistakably in the afternoon sun. Yet, he pulled away.

Her lips hungered and her breasts ached—and *he* was walking away again, in spite of all he'd said about how much he wanted her. This man confused the hell out of her.

Five days later, Shannon lounged on the downstairs lanai and watched her son drive along the beach in his miniature Jeep, dogs romping alongside. This was the first time she'd been left to her own devices in days. She'd never been romanced so thoroughly in her life. True to his word, over the past week Tony had been at his most charming.

Could her time here already be almost over?

Sipping freshly squeezed lemonade—although the drink tasted far too amazing for such a simple name—she savored the tart taste. Of course everything seemed sharper, crisper as tension seeped from her bones. The concerns of the world felt forever away while the sun warmed her skin and the waves provided a soothing sound track to her days.

And she had Tony to thank for it all. She'd never known there were so many entertainment options on an island. Of course Enrique Medina had spared no expense in building his compound.

A movie screening room with all the latest films piped in for private viewing.

Three different dining rooms for everything from family style to white-tie.

Rec room, gym, indoor and outdoor swimming pools.

She could still hear Kolby's squeal of delight over the stable of horses and ponies.

Throughout it all, Tony had been at her side with tantalizing brushes of his strong body against hers. All the while his rich chocolate brown eyes reminded Shannon that the next move was up to her. Not that they stood a chance at finding privacy today. The grounds buzzed with activity, and today, no sign of Tony.

Behind her, the doors snicked open. Tony? Her heart stuttered a quick syncopation as she glanced back.

Alys walked toward her, high heels clicking on the tiled veranda as she angled past two guards comparing notes on their twin BlackBerry phones. Shannon forced herself to keep the smile in place. It would be rude to frown in disappointment, especially after how helpful the woman had been.

Too bad the disappointment wasn't as easy to hide from herself. No doubt about it, Tony was working his way back into her life.

The king's assistant stopped at the fully stocked outdoor bar and poured a glass of lemonade from the crystal pitcher.

Shannon thumbed the condensation on the cold glass. "Is there something you need?"

"Antonio wanted me to find you, and I have." She tapped her silver BlackBerry attached to the waistband of her linen skirt. Ever crisp with her power suit and French manicure. As usual the elegant woman didn't have a wrinkle in sight, much less wince over working in heels all day. "He'll be out shortly. He's finishing up a meeting with his father."

"I should get Kolby." She swung her feet to the side.

How silly to be glad she'd caved and used some of the new clothes. She had worn everything she brought with her twice and while the laundry service easily kept up with her limited wardrobe, she'd begun to feel a little ungrateful not to wear at least a few of the things that someone had gone to a lot of trouble to provide. Shannon smoothed the de la Renta scoop-necked dress, the fabric so decadently soft it caressed her skin with every move.

"No need to stop the boy's fun just yet. Antonio is on his way." Alys perched on the edge of the lounger, glass on her knee.

Shannon rubbed the hem of her dress between two fingers much like Kolby with his blanket when he needed soothing. "I hear you're the one who ordered all the new clothes. Thank you."

Alys saw to everything else in this smoothly run place. "No need for thanks. It's my job."

"You have excellent taste." She tugged the hem back over her knees.

"I saw your photo online and chose things that would flatter your frame and coloring. It's fun to shop on someone else's dime."

More than a dime had gone into this wardrobe. Her closet sported new additions each morning. Everything from casual jeans and designer blouses to silky dresses and heels to wear for dinner. An assortment of bathing suits to choose from....

And the lingerie. A decadent shiver slid down her spine at the feel of the fine silks and satins against her skin. Although it made her uncomfortable to think of this woman choosing everything.

Alys turned her glass around and around on her knee. "The expense you worry about is nothing to them. They can afford the finest. It would bother them to see you struggling. Now you fit in and that gives the king less to worry about."

God forbid her tennis shoes should make the king uncomfortable. But saying as much would make her sound ungrateful, so she toyed with her glasses, pulling them off and cleaning them with her napkin even though they were already crystal clear. The dynamics of this place went beyond any household she'd ever seen. Alys seemed more comfortable here than Tony.

Shannon slid her glasses back on. "If you don't mind my asking, how long have you been working for the king?"

"Only three months."

How long did she intend to stay? The island was luxurious, but in more of a vacation kind of way. It was so cut off from the world, time seemed to stand still. What kind of life could the woman build in this place?

Abruptly, Alys leaped to her feet. "Here is Antonio now."

He charged confidently through the door, eyes locked on Shannon. "Thank you for finding her, Alys."

The assistant backed away. "Of course." Alys stepped out of hearing range, giving them some privacy.

Forking a hand through his hair—messing up the precise combing from his conference with his father—Tony wore a suit without a tie. The jacket perhaps a nod toward meeting with his father? His smile was carefree, but his shoulders bore the extra tension she'd come to realize accompanied time he had spent with the king.

"How did your meeting go?"

"Don't want to talk about that." Tony plucked a lily from the vase on the bar, snapped the stem off and tucked the bloom behind her ear. "Would much rather enjoy the view. The flower is almost as gorgeous as you are."

The lush perfume filled each breath. "All the fresh flowers are positively decadent."

"I wish I could take credit, but there's a hothouse with a supply that's virtually unlimited."

Yet another amenity she wouldn't have guessed, although it certainly explained all the fresh-cut flowers. "Still," she repeated as she touched the lily tucked in her hair, "I appreciate the gesture."

"I would make love to you on a bed of flowers if you let me." He thumbed her earlobe lightly before skimming his knuckles along her collarbone.

How easy it would be to give over to the delicious seduction of his words and his world. Except she'd allowed herself to fall into that trap before.

And of course there was that little technicality that *he* had been the one holding back all week. "What about thorns?"

He laughed, his hand falling away from her skin and palming her back. "Come on, my practical love. We're going out."

Love? She swallowed to dampen her suddenly cottony mouth. "To lunch?"

"To the airstrip."

Her stomach lurched. This slice of time away was over already? "We're leaving?"

"Not that lucky, I'm afraid. Your apartment is still staked out with the press and curious royalty groupie types. You may want to consider a gated community on top of the added security measures. I know the cost freaks you out, but give my lawyer another couple of days to work on those restraining orders and we can take it from there. As for where we're going today, we're greeting guests and I'd like you to come along."

They weren't leaving. Relief sang through her so intensely it gave her pause.

Tony cocked his head to the side. "Would you like to come with me?"

"Uh, yes, I think so." She struggled to gather her scrambled thoughts and composure. "I just need to settle Kolby."

Alys cleared her throat a few feet away. "I've already notified Miss Delgado, the younger nanny. She's ordering a picnic lunch and bringing sand toys. Then of course she will watch over him during his naptime if needed. I assume that's acceptable to you?"

Her son would enjoy that more than a car ride and waiting around for the flight. She was growing quite spoiled having afternoons completely free while Kolby napped safely under a nanny's watchful care. "Of course. That sounds perfect."

Shannon smiled her thanks and reached out to touch the woman's arm. Except Alys wasn't looking at her. The king's assistant had her eyes firmly planted elsewhere.

On Tony.

Shock nailed her feet to the tiles. Then a fierce jealousy vibrated through her, a feeling that was most definitely ugly and not her style. She'd thought herself above such a primitive emotion, not to mention Tony hadn't given the woman any encouragement.

Still, Shannon fought the urge to link her arm with his in a great big "mine" statement. In that unguarded moment, Alys revealed clearly what she hoped to gain from living here.

Alys wanted a Medina man.

Eight

Tony guided the Porsche Cayenne four-wheel drive along the island road toward the airstrip, glad Shannon was with him to ease the edge on the upcoming meeting. Although having her with him brought a special torment all its own.

The past week working his way back into her good graces had been a painful pleasure, sharpening the razor edge on his need to have her in his bed again. Spending time with her had only shown him more reasons to want her. She mesmerized him with the simplest things.

When she sat on the pool edge and kicked her feet through the water, he thought of those long legs wrapped around him.

Seeing her sip a glass of lemonade made him ache to taste the tart fruit on her lips.

The way she cleaned her glasses with a gust of breath

fogging the frames made him think of her panting in his ear as he brought her to completion.

Romancing his way back into her good graces was easier said than done. And the goal of it all made each day on this island easier to bear.

And after they returned to Galveston? He would face that then. Right now, he had more of his father's past to deal with.

"Tony?" Bracing her hand against the dash as the rutted road challenged even the quality shock absorbers, she looked so right sitting in the seat next to him. "You still haven't told me who we're picking up. Your brothers, perhaps?"

Steering the SUV under the arch of palm trees lining both sides of the road, he searched for the right words to prepare Shannon for something he'd never shared with a soul. "You're on the right track." His hands gripped the steering wheel tighter. "My sister. Half sister, actually. Eloisa."

"A sister? I didn't know…."

"Neither does the press." His half sister had stayed under the radar, growing up with her mother and stepfather in Pensacola, Florida. Only recently had Eloisa reestablished contact with their father. "She's coming here to regroup, troubleshoot. Prepare. Now that the Medina secret is out, her story will also be revealed soon enough."

"May I ask what that story might be?"

"Of course." He focused on the two-lane road, a convenient excuse to make sure she didn't see any anger pushing past his boundaries. "My father had a relationship with her mother after arriving in the U.S., which resulted in Eloisa. She's in her mid-twenties now."

Shannon's eyes went wide behind her glasses.

"Yeah, I know." Turning, he drove from the jungle road

onto a waterside route leading to the ferry station. "That's a tight timeline between when we left San Rinaldo and the hookup." Tight timeline in regard to his mother's death.

"That must have been confusing for you. Kolby barely remembers his father and it's been tough for him to accept you. And we haven't had to deal with adding another child to the mix."

A child? With Shannon? An image of a dark-haired baby—his baby—in her arms blindsided him, derailing his thoughts away from his father in a flash. His foot slid off the accelerator. Shaking free of the image was easier said than done as it grew roots in his mind—Kolby stepping into the picture until a family portrait took shape.

God, just last week he'd been thinking how he knew nothing about kids. She was the one hinting at marriage, not him. Although she said the opposite until he didn't know what was up.

Things with Shannon weren't as simple as he'd planned at the outset. "My father's affair was his own business."

"Okay, then." She pulled her glasses off and fogged them with her breath. She dried them with the hem of her dress. "Do you and your sister get along?"

He hauled his eyes from Shannon's glasses before he swerved off onto the beach. Or pulled onto the nearest side road and to hell with making it to the airstrip on time.

"I've only met her once before." When Tony was a teenager. His father had gone all out on that lone visit with his seven-year-old daughter. Tony didn't resent Eloisa. It wasn't her fault, after all. In fact, he grew even more pissed off at his father. Enrique had responsibilities to his daughter. If he wanted to stay out of her life, then fine. Do so. But half measures were bull.

Yet wasn't that what he'd been offering Shannon? Half measures?

Self-realization sucked. "She's come here on her own since then. She and Duarte have even met up a few times, which in a roundabout way brought on the media mess."

"How so?" She slid her glasses back in place.

"Our sister married into a high-profile family. Eloisa's husband is the son of an ambassador and brother to a senator. He's a Landis."

She sat up straighter at the mention of America's political royalty. Talk about irony.

Tony slowed for a fuel truck to pass. "The Landis name naturally comes with media attention." He accelerated into the parking lot alongside the ferry station, the boat already close to shore. An airplane was parked on the distant airstrip. "Her husband—Jonah—likes to keep a low profile, but that's just not possible."

"What happened?"

"Duarte was delivering one of our father's messages, which put him on a collision course with a press camera. We're still trying to figure out how the Global Intruder made the connection. Although, it's a moot point now. Every stray photo of all of us has been unearthed, every detail of our pasts."

"Of my past?" Her face drained of color.

"I'm afraid so."

All the more reason for her to stay on the island. Her husband's illegal dealings, even his suicide, had hit the headlines again this morning, thanks to muckrakers looking for more scandal connected to the Medina story. He would only be able to shield Shannon from that for so long. She had a right to know.

"I've grown complacent this week." She pressed a hand to her stomach. "My poor in-laws."

The SUV idled in the parking spot, the ferry already

preparing to dock. He didn't have much time left alone with her.

Tony skimmed back her silky blond hair. "I'm sorry all this has come up again. And I hate it that I can't do more to fix things for you."

Turning toward his touch, she rested her face in his hand. "You've helped this week."

He wanted to kiss her, burned to recline the seats and explore the hint of cleavage in her scoop-necked dress. And damned if that wasn't exactly what he planned to do.

Slanting his mouth over her, he caught her gasp and took full advantage of her parted lips with a determined sweep of his tongue. Need for her pumped through his veins, fast-tracked blood from his head to his groin until he could only feel, smell, taste undiluted *Shannon*. Her gasp quickly turned to a sigh as she melted against him, the curves of her breasts pressed to his chest, her fingernails digging deeply into his forearms as she urged him closer.

He was more than happy to accommodate.

It had been so long, too long since they'd had sex before their argument over his damned money. Nearly fourteen days that seemed like fourteen years since he'd had his hands on her this way, fully and unrestrained, tunneling under her clothes, reacquainting himself with the perfection of her soft skin and perfect curves. She fit against him with a rightness he knew extended even further with their clothes off. A hitch in her throat, the flush rising on the exposed curve of her breasts keyed him in to her rising need, as if he couldn't already tell by the way she nearly crawled across the seat to get closer.

Shannon wanted sex with him every bit as much as he wanted her. But that required privacy, not a parking lot in clear view of the approaching ferry.

Holding back now was the right move, even if it was killing him.

"Come on. Time to meet my sister." He slid out of her arms and the SUV and around to her door before she could shuffle her purse from her lap to her shoulder.

He opened the door and she smiled her thanks without speaking, yet another thing he appreciated about her. She sensed when he didn't want to talk anymore. He'd shared things with women over the years, but until her, he'd never found one with whom he could share silence.

The lapping waves, the squawk of gulls, the endless stretch of water centered him, steadying his steps and reminding him how to keep his balance in a rocky world.

Resting his head on Shannon's back, he waited while the ferry finished docking. His sister and her husband stood at the railing. Eloisa's husband hooked an arm around her shoulders, the couple talking intently.

Eloisa might not be a carbon copy of their father, but she carried an air of something unmistakably Medina about her. His father had once said she looked like their grandmother. Tony wouldn't know, since he couldn't remember his grandparents who'd all died before he was born.

The loudspeaker blared with the boat captain announcing their arrival. Disembarking, the couple stayed close together, his brother-in-law broadcasting a protective air. Jonah was the unconventional Landis, according to the papers. If so, they should get along just fine.

The couple stepped from the boat to the dock, and up close Eloisa didn't appear nearly as calm as from a distance. Lines of strain showed in her eyes.

"Welcome," Tony said. "Eloisa, Jonah, this is Shannon Crawford, and I'm—"

"Antonio, I know." His sister spoke softly, reserved. "I recognize you both from the papers."

He'd met Eloisa once as a child when she'd visited the island. She'd come back recently, but he'd been long gone by then.

They were strangers and relatives. Awkward, to say the least.

Jonah Landis stepped up. "Glad you could accommodate our request for a visit so quickly."

"Damage control is important."

Eloisa simply took his hand, searching his face. "How's our father?"

"Not well." Had Shannon just stepped closer to him? Tony kept his eyes forward, knowing in his gut he would see sympathy in her eyes. "He says his doctors are doing all they can."

Blinking back tears, Eloisa stood straighter with a willowy strength. "I barely know him, but I can't envision a world without him in it. Sounds crazy, I'm sure."

He understood too well. Making peace was hard as hell, yet somehow she seemed to have managed.

Jonah clapped him on the back. "Well, my new bro, I need to grab Eloisa's bags and meet you at the car."

A Landis who carried his own luggage? Tony liked the unpretentious guy already.

And wasn't that one of the things he liked most about Shannon? Her down-to-earth ways in spite of her wealthy lifestyle with her husband. She seemed completely unimpressed with the Medina money, much less his defunct title.

For the first time he considered she might be right. She may be better off without the strain of his messed-up family.

Which made him a selfish bastard for pursuing her. But

he couldn't seem to pull back now when his world had been rocked on its foundation. The sailor in him recognized the only port in the storm, and right now, only a de la Renta dress separated him from what he wanted—needed—more than anything.

However, he needed to choose his time and place carefully with the private island growing more crowded by the minute.

The next afternoon, Shannon sat beside Tony in the Porsche four-wheel drive on the way to the beach. He'd left her a note to put on her bathing suit and meet him during Kolby's naptime. She'd been taken aback at the leap of excitement in her stomach over spending time alone with him.

The beach road took them all the way to the edge of the shoreline. He shifted the car in Park, his legs flexing in black board shorts as he left the car silently. He'd been quiet for the whole drive, and she didn't feel the need to fill the moment with aimless babbling. Being together and quiet had an appeal all its own.

Tugging on the edge of the white cover-up, she eyed the secluded stretch of beach. Could this be the end of the "romancing" and the shift back to intimacy? Her stomach fluttered faster.

She stepped from the car before he could open her door. Wind ruffled his hair and whipped his shorts, low slung on his hips. She knew his body well but still the muscled hardness hitched her breath in her throat. Bronzed and toned—smart, rich and royal to boot. Life had handed him an amazing hand, and yet he still chose to work insane hours. In fact, she'd spent more time with him this past week than during the months they'd dated in Galveston.

And everything she learned confused her more than solving questions.

She jammed her hands in the pockets of her cover-up. "Are you going to tell me why we're here?"

"Over there." He pointed to a cluster of palm trees with surfboards propped and waiting.

"You're kidding, right? Tony, I don't surf, and the water must be cold."

"You'll warm up. The waves aren't high enough today for surfing. But there're still some things even a beginner can do." He peeled off his T-shirt and she realized she was staring, damn it. "You won't break anything. Trust me."

He extended a hand.

Trust? Easier said than done. She eyed the boards and looked back at him. They were on the island, she reminded herself, removed from real life. And bottom line, while she wasn't sure she trusted him with her heart, she totally trusted him with her body. He wouldn't let anything happen to her.

Decision made, she whipped her cover-up over her head, revealing her crocheted swimsuit. His eyes flamed over her before he took her cover-up and tossed it in the SUV along with his T-shirt. He closed his hands around hers in a warm steady grip and started toward the boards.

She eyed the pair propped against trees—obviously set up in advance for their outing. One shiny and new, bright white with tropical flowers around the edges. The other was simpler, just yellow, faded from time and use. She looked at the water again, starting to have second—

"Hey." He squeezed her hand. "We're just going to paddle out. Nothing too adventurous today, but I think you're going to find even slow and steady has some unexpected thrills."

And didn't that send her heart double timing?

Thank goodness he moved quickly. Mere minutes later she was on her stomach, on the board, paddling away from shore to…nowhere. Nothing but aqua blue waters blending into a paler sky. Mild waves rolled beneath her but somehow never lifted her high enough to be scary, more of a gentle rocking. The chilly water turned to a neutral sluice over her body, soothing her into becoming one with the ocean.

One stroke at a time she let go of goals and racing to the finish line. Her life had been on fast-paced frenetic since Nolan died. Now, for the first time in longer than she could remember, she was able to unwind, almost hypnotized by the dip, dip, dip of her hands and Tony's into the water.

Tension she hadn't even realized kinked her muscles began to ease. Somehow, Tony must have known. She turned her head to thank him and found him staring back at her.

She threaded her fingers through the water, sun baking her back. "It's so quiet out here."

"I thought you would appreciate the time away."

"You were right." She slowed her paddling and just floated. "You've given over a lot of your time to make sure Kolby and I stayed entertained. Don't you need to get back to work?"

"I work from the island using my computer and telecoms." His hair, even darker when wet, was slicked back from his face, his damp skin glinting in the sun. "More and more of business is being conducted that way."

"Do you ever sleep?"

"Not so much lately, but that has nothing to do with work." He held her with his eyes locked on her face, no suggestive body sweep, just intense, undiluted Tony.

And she couldn't help but wonder why he went to so much trouble when they weren't sleeping together anymore.

If his conscience bothered him, he could have assigned guards to watch over her and she wouldn't have argued for Kolby's sake. Yet here he was. With her.

"What do you see in me?" She rested her cheek on her folded hands. "I'm not fishing for compliments, honest to God, it's just we seem so wrong for each other on so many levels. Is it just the challenge, like building your business?"

"Shanny, you take *challenge* to a whole 'nother level."

She flicked water in his face. "I'm being serious here. No joking around, please."

"Seriously?" He stared out at the horizon for a second as if gathering his thoughts. "Since you brought up the business analogy, let's run with that. At work you would be someone I want on my team. Your tenacity, your refusal to give up—even your frustrating rejection of my help— impress the hell out of me. You're an amazing woman, so much so that sometimes I can't even look away."

He made her feel strong and special with a few words. After feeling guilty for so long, of wondering if she could hold it all together for Kolby, she welcomed the reassurance coursing through her veins as surely as the current underneath her.

Tony slid from his board and ducked under. She watched through the clear surface as he freed the ankle leash attaching him to his board.

Resurfacing beside her, he stroked the line of her back. "Sit up for a minute."

"What?" She'd barely heard him, too focused on the feel of his hand low on her waist.

"Sit up on the board and swing your legs over the side." He held the edge. "I won't let you fall."

"But your board's drifting." She watched the faded yellow inch away.

"I'll get it later. Come on." He palmed her back, helping her balance as finally, she wriggled her way upright.

She bobbled. Stifled a squeal. Then realized what was the worst that could happen? She would be in the water. Big deal. And suddenly the surfboard steadied a little, still rocking but not out of control. The waters lapped around her legs, cool, exciting.

"I did it." She laughed, sending her voice out into that endlessness.

"Perfect. Now hold still," he said and somehow slid effortlessly behind her.

Her balance went haywire again for a second, the horizon tilting until she was sure they would both topple over.

"Relax," he said against her ear. "Out here, it's not about fighting, it's the one place you can totally let go."

The one place *he* could let go? And suddenly she realized this was about more than getting her to relax. He was sharing something about himself with her. Even a man as driven and successful as himself needed a break from the demands of everyday life. Perhaps because of moments like these he kept it all together rather than letting the tension tighten until it snapped.

She fit herself against him, his legs behind hers as they drifted. Her muscles slowly melted until she leaned into him. The waves curled underneath, his chest wet and bristly against her skin. A new tension coiled inside her, deep in her belly. Her swimsuit suddenly felt too tight against her breasts that swelled and yearned for the brush of the air and Tony's mouth.

His palms rested on her thighs. His thumbs circled a light massage, close, so close. Water ebbed and flowed over her heated core, waves sweeping tantalizing caresses on her aching flesh. Her head sagged onto his shoulder.

With each undulation of the board, he rocked against her, stirring, growing harder until he pressed fully erect along her spine. Every roll of the board rubbing their bodies against each other had to be as torturous for him as it was for her. His hands moved higher on her legs, nearer to what she needed. Silently. Just as in tune with each other as when they'd been paddling out.

She worried at first that someone might see, but with their backs to the shore and water…she could lose herself in the moment. Already his breaths grew heavier against her ear, nearly as fast as her own.

They could both let go and find completion right here without ever moving. Simply feeling his arousal against her stirred Shannon to a bittersweet edge. And good God, that scared the hell out of her.

The wind chilled, and she recognized the sting of fear all too well. She'd thought she could ride the wave, so to speak, and just have an affair with Tony.

But this utter abandon, the loss of control, the way they were together, it was anything but simple, something she wasn't sure she was ready to risk.

Scavenging every bit of her quickly dwindling willpower, she grabbed his wrists, moved his hands away…

And dived off the side of the board.

Nine

Tony propped his surfboard against a tree and turned to take Shannon's. The wariness in her eyes frustrated the hell out of him. He could have sworn she was just as into the moment out there as he was—an amazing moment that had been seconds away from getting even better.

And then she'd vaulted off the board and into the water.

Staying well clear of him, she'd said she was ready to return to shore. She hadn't spoken another word since. Had he blown a whole week's worth of working past her boundaries only to wreck it in one afternoon? Problem was, he still didn't know what had set her off.

She stroked a smudge of sand from his faded yellow board. "Is it all right to leave them here so far from where we started?"

They'd drifted at least a mile from the SUV. "I'll buy new ones. I'm a filthy rich prince, remember?"

Yeah, sexual frustration was making him a little cranky, and he suspected no amount of walking would take the edge off. Worse yet, she didn't even rise to the bait of his crabby words full of reminders of why they'd broken up in the first place.

Fine. Who the hell knew what she needed?

He started west and she glided alongside him. The wind picked up, rustling the trees and sweeping a layer of sand around his ankles.

Shannon gasped.

"What?" Tony looked fast. "Did you step on something? Are you getting chilly?"

Shaking her head, she pointed toward the trees, branches and leaves sweeping apart to reveal the small stone chapel. "Why didn't I notice that when we drove here?"

"We approached the beach from a different angle."

"It's gorgeous." Her eyes were wide and curious.

"No need to look so surprised. I told you that we lived here 24/7. My father outfitted the island with everything we would need, from a small medical clinic to that church." He took in the white stone church, mission bell over the front doors. It wasn't large, but big enough to accommodate everyone here. His older brother had told him once it was the only thing on the island built to resemble a part of their old life.

"Were you an altar server?"

Her voice pulled him back to the present.

"With a short-lived tenure." He glanced down at her, so damn glad she was talking to him again. "I couldn't sit still and the priest frowned on an altar server bringing a bag of books and Legos to keep himself entertained during the service."

"Legos?" She started walking again. "Really?"

"Every Sunday as I sat out in the congregation. I would

have brought more, but the nanny confiscated my squirt gun."

"Don't be giving Kolby any ideas." She elbowed him lightly, then as if realizing what she'd done, picked up her pace.

Hell no, he wasn't losing ground that fast. "The nanny didn't find my knife though."

Her mouth dropped open. "You brought a knife to church?"

"I carved my initials under the pew. Wanna go see if they're still there?"

She eyed the church, then shook her head. "What's all this about today? The surfing and then stories about Legos?"

Why? He hadn't stopped to consider the reasons, just acting on instinct to keep up with the crazy, out-of-control relationship with Shannon. But he didn't do things without a reason.

His gut had pointed him in this direction because… "So that you remember there's a man in here." He thumped his chest. "As well as a filthy rich prince."

But no matter what he said or how far he got from this place, the Medina heritage coursed through his veins. Regardless of how many times he changed his name or started over, he was still Antonio Medina. And Shannon had made it clear time and time again, she didn't want that kind of life. Finally, he heard her.

Several hours later, Shannon shoved her head deeper into the industrial sized refrigerator in search of a midnight snack. A glass of warm milk just wasn't going to cut it.

Eyeing the plate of *trufas con cognac* and small cups of *crema catalana,* she debated whether to go for the brandy truffles or cold custard with caramel on top.... She picked one of each and dropped into a seat at the steel table.

Silence bounced and echoed in the cavernous kitchen. She was sleepy and cranky and edgy. And it was all Tony's fault for tormenting her with charming stories and sexy encounters on the water—then shutting her out. She nipped an edge of the liqueur-flavored chocolate. Amazing. Sighing, she sagged back in the chair.

Since returning from their surfing outing, he'd kept his distance. She'd thought they were getting closer on a deeper level when he'd shared about his sister and even the Lego, then, wham. He'd turned into the perfect—distant—host at the stilted family dinner.

Not that she'd been able to eat a bite.

Now, she was hungry, in spite of the fact she'd finished off the truffle. She spooned a scoop of custard into her mouth, although she suspected no amount of gourmet pastries would satisfy the craving gnawing her inside.

When she'd started dating Tony, she'd taken a careful, calculated risk because her hormones had been hollering for him and she'd been a long, long time without sex. Okay, so her hormones hadn't been shouting for just any man. Only Tony. A problem that didn't seem to have abated in the least.

"Ah, hell." Tony's low curse startled her upright in her seat.

Filling the archway, he studied her cautiously. He wore jeans and an open button-down that appeared hastily tossed on. He fastened two buttons in the middle, slowly shielding the cut of his six-pack abs.

Cool custard melted in her mouth, her senses singing. But her heart was aching and confused. She toyed with the neck of her robe nervously. The blue peignoir set covered her from neck to toes, but the loose-fitting chiffon and lace brushed sensual decadence against her skin. The froufrou little kitten heels to match had seemed over-the-top in her room, but now felt sexy and fun.

Her hands shook. She pressed them against the steel topped table. "Don't mind me. I'm just indulging in a midnight feeding frenzy. I highly recommend the custard cups in the back right corner of the refrigerator."

He hesitated in the archway as if making up his mind, then walked deeper into the kitchen, passing her without touching. "I was thinking in terms of something more substantial, like a sandwich."

"Are princes allowed to make their own snacks?"

"Who's going to tell me no?" He kicked the fridge closed, his hands full of deli meat, cheese and lettuce, a jar of spread tucked under his elbow.

"Good point." She swirled another spoonful. "I hope the cook doesn't mind I've been foraging around. I actually used the stove, too, when I cooked a late night snack for Kolby. He woke up hungry."

Tony glanced over from his sandwich prep. "Is he okay?"

"Just a little homesick." Her eyes took in the sight of the Tony she remembered, a man who wore jeans low-slung on his hips. And rumpled hair…she enjoyed the disobedient swirls in his hair most.

"I'm sorry for that." His shoulders tensed under the loose chambray.

"Don't get me wrong, I appreciate how everyone has gone out of their way for him. The gourmet kid cuisine makes meals an adventure. I wish I had thought to tell him rolled tortillas are snakes and caterpillars." Pasta was called worms or a nest. "I'm even becoming addicted to Nutella crepes. But sometimes, a kid just needs the familiar feel of home."

"I understand." His sandwich piled high on a plate, he took a seat—across from her rather than beside as he would have in the past.

"Of course you do." She clenched her hands together to keep from reaching out to him. "Well, I'll have to make sure the cook knows I tried to put everything back where I found it."

"He's more likely to be upset that you called him a cook rather than a chef."

"Ah, a chef. Right. All those nuances between your world and mine." How surreal to be having a conversation with a prince over a totally plebian hoagie.

Tony swiped at his mouth with a linen napkin and draped it over his knee again. "You ran in a pretty high-finance world with your husband."

Her husband's dirty money.

She shoved away the custard bowl. Thoughts of the media regurgitating that mess for public consumption made her nauseated. She wasn't close to her in-laws, but they would suffer hearing their precious son's reputation smeared again.

And God help them all if her own secrets were somehow discovered.

Best to lie low and keep to herself. Although she was finding it increasingly difficult to imagine how she would restart her life. Even if she was able to renew her teaching credentials, who was going to want to hire the infamous Medina Mistress who'd once been married to a crook? When this mess was over, she would have to dig deep to figure out how to recreate a life for herself and Kolby.

Could Tony be having second thoughts about their relationship? His strict code of honor would dictate he take care of her until the media storm passed, but she didn't want to be his duty.

They'd dated. They'd had sex. But she only just realized how much of their relationship had been superficial as they both dodged discussing deeper, darker parts of their past.

Still, she wasn't ready to plunge into the murkiest of waters that made up her life with Nolan. She wasn't even sure right now if Tony would want to hear.

But regardless of how things turned out between them, she needed him to understand the real her. "I didn't grow up with all those trappings of Nolan's world. My dad was a high school science teacher and a coach. My mom was the elementary school secretary. We had enough money, but we were by no means wealthy." She hesitated, realizing… "You probably already know all of that."

"Why would you think so?" he asked, although he hadn't denied what she said.

"If you've had to be so worried about security and your identity, it makes sense you or your lawyer or some security team you've hired would vet people in your life."

"That would be the wise thing to do."

"And you're a smart man."

"I haven't always acted wisely around you."

"You've been a perfect gentleman this week and you know it," she said, as close as she could come to hinting that she ached for his touch, his mouth on her body, the familiar rise of pleasure and release he could bring.

Tony shrugged and tore into his sandwich again, a grandfather clock tolling once in the background.

"Kolby thinks we're on vacation."

"Good." He finished chewing, tendons in his strong neck flexing. "That's how he should remember this time in his life."

"It's unreal how you and your father have shielded him from the tension in your relationship."

"Obviously not well enough to fool you." His boldly handsome face gave nothing away.

"I know some about your history, and it's tough to miss how little the two of you talk. Your father's an interesting man." She'd enjoyed after-dinner discussions with Enrique and Eloisa about current events and the latest book they'd read.

The old king may have isolated himself from the world, but he'd certainly stayed abreast with the latest news. The discussions had been enlightening on a number of levels, such as how the old king wasn't as clipped and curt with his daughter as he was with Tony.

Tony stared at the last half of his snack, tucking a straggly piece of lettuce back inside. "What did you make for Kolby?"

His question surprised her, but if it kept him talking…

"French toast. It's one of his favorite comfort foods. He likes for me to cut the toast into slices so he can dip it into the syrup. Independence means a lot, even to a three-year-old." It meant a lot to adults. She reached for her bowl to scrape the final taste of custard and licked the spoon clean. The caramel taste exploded into her starving senses like music in her mouth.

Pupils widening with awareness until they nearly pushed away his brown irises, Tony stared back at her across the table, intense, aroused. Her body recognized the signs in him well even if he didn't move so much as an inch closer.

She set the spoon down, the tiny clink echoing in the empty kitchen. "Tony, why are you still awake?"

"I'm a night owl. Some might call me an insomniac."

"An insomniac? I didn't know that." She laughed darkly. "Although how could I since we've never spent an entire night together? Have you had the problem long?"

"I've always been this way." He turned the plate around on the table. "My mother tried everything from warm milk to a 'magic' blanket before just letting me stay up. She used to cook for me too, late at night."

"Your mother, the queen, cooked?" She inched to the edge of her chair, leaning on her elbows, hoping to hold his attention and keep him talking.

"She may have been royalty even before she married my father, but there are plenty in Europe with blue blood and little money." Shadows chased each other across his eyes. "My mother grew up learning the basics of managing her own house. She insisted we boys have run of the kitchen. There were so many everyday places that were off-limits to us for safety reasons, she wanted us to have the normalcy of popping in and out of the kitchen for snacks."

Like any other child. A child who happened to live in a sixteenth-century castle. She liked his mother, a woman she would never meet but felt so very close to at the moment. "What did she cook for you?"

"A Cyclops."

"Excuse me?"

"It's a fried egg with a buttered piece of bread on top." He swirled his hand over his plate as if he could spin an image into reality. "The bread has a hole pinched out of the middle so the egg yolk peeks out like a—"

"Like a Cyclops. I see. My mom called it a Popeye." And with the memory of a simple egg dish, she felt the connection to Tony spin and gain strength again.

He glanced up, a half smile kicking into his one cheek. "Cyclops appealed to the bloodthirsty little boy in me. Just like Kolby and the caterpillar and snake pasta."

To hell with distance and waiting for him to reach out, she covered his hand with hers. "Your mother sounds wonderful."

He nodded briefly. "I believe she was."

"Believe?"

"I have very few memories of her before she…died." He turned his hand over and stroked hers with his thumb. "The beach. A blanket. Food."

"Scents do tend to anchor our memories more firmly."

More shadows drifted through his eyes, darker this time, like storm clouds. *Died* seemed such a benign word to describe the assassination of a young mother, killed because she'd married a king. A vein pulsed visibly in Tony's temple, faster by the second. He'd dealt with such devastating circumstances in life honorably, while her husband had turned to stealing and finally, to taking the ultimate coward's way out.

She held herself very still, unthreatening. Her heart ached for him on a whole new and intense level. "What do you remember about when she died? About leaving San Rinaldo?"

"Not much really." He stayed focused on their connected hands, tracing the veins on her wrist with exaggerated concentration. "I was only five."

So he'd told her before. But she wasn't buying his nonchalance. "Traumatic events seem to stick more firmly in our memory. I recall a car accident when I couldn't have been more than two." She wouldn't back down now, not when she was so close to understanding the man behind the smiles and bold gestures. "I still remember the bright red of the Volkswagen bug."

"You probably saw pictures of the car later," he said dismissively, then looked up sharply, aggressively full of bravado. The storm clouds churned faster with each throb of the vein on his temple. He stroked up her arm with unmistakable sensual intent. "How much longer are you going to wait before you ask me to kiss you again? Because right now, I'm so on fire for you, I want to test out the sturdiness of that table."

"Tony, can you even hear yourself?" she asked, frustrated and even a bit insulted by the way he was jerking her around. "One minute you're Prince Romance and Restraint, the next you're ignoring me over dinner. Then you're spilling your guts. Now, you proposition me—and not too suavely, I might add. Quite frankly, you're giving me emotional whiplash."

His arms twitched, thick roped muscles bulging against his sleeves with restrained power. "Make no mistake, I have wanted you every second of every day. It's all I can do not to haul you against me right now and to hell with the dozens of people that might walk in. But today on the water and tonight here, I'm just not sure this crazy life of mine is good enough for you."

Her body burned in response to his words even as her mind blared a warning. Tony had felt the increasing connection too, and it scared him. So he'd tried to run her off with the crude offer of sex on the table.

Well too damn bad for him, she wasn't backing down. She'd wanted this, *him,* for too long to turn away.

Ten

He'd wanted Shannon back in his bed, but somewhere between making a sandwich and talking about eggs, she'd peeled away walls, exposing thoughts and memories that were better forgotten. They distracted. Hurt. Served no damn purpose.

Anger grated his raw insides. "So? What'll it be? Sex here or in your room?"

She didn't flinch and she didn't leave. Her soft hand stayed on top of his as she looked at him with sad eyes behind her glasses. "Is that what this week has been about?"

He let his gaze linger on the vee of her frothy nightgown set. Lace along the neckline traced into the curve of her breasts the way his hands ached to explore. "I've been clear from the start about what I want."

"Are you so sure about that?"

"What the hell is that supposed to mean?" he snapped.

Sliding from her chair, she circled the table toward him, her heels clicking against the tile. She stopped beside him, the hem of her nightgown set swirling against his leg. "Don't confuse me with your mother."

"Good God, there's not a chance of that." He toppled her into his lap and lowered his head, determined to prove it to her.

"Wait." She stopped him with a hand flattened to his chest just above the two closed buttons. Her palm cooled his overheated skin, calming and stirring, but then she'd always been a mix of contradictions. "You suffered a horrible trauma as a child. No one should lose a parent, especially in such an awful way. I wish you could have been spared that."

"I wish my *mother* had been spared." His hands clenched in her robe, his fists against her back.

"And I can't help but wonder if you helping me—a mother with a young child—is a way to put her ghost to rest. Putting your own ghosts to rest in the process."

Given the crap that had shaken down in his past, he'd done a fine job turning his life around. Frustration poured acid on his burning gut. "You've spent a lot of time thinking about this."

"What you told me this afternoon and tonight brought things into focus."

"Well, thanks for the psychoanalysis." His words came out harsh, but right now he needed her to walk away. "I would offer to pay you for the services, but I wouldn't want to start another fight."

"Sounds to me like you're spoiling for one now." Her eyes softened with more of that concern that grated along his insides. "I'm sorry if I overstepped and hit a nerve."

A nerve? She'd performed a root canal on his emotions. His brain echoed with the retort of gunfire stuttering, aimed at him, his brothers. His mother. He searched for what to say to shut down this conversation, but he wasn't sure of anything other than his need for a serious, body-draining jog on the beach. Problem was? The beach circled right back around to this place.

Easing from his lap, she stood and he tamped down the swift kick of disappointment. Except she didn't leave. She extended her hand and linked her fingers with his.

Just a simple connection, but since he was raw to the core, her touch fired deep.

"Shannon," he said between teeth clenched tight with restraint, "I'm about a second from snapping here. So unless you want me buried heart deep inside you in the next two minutes, you need to go back to your room."

Her hold stayed firm, cool and steady.

"Shannon, damn it all, you don't know what you're doing. You don't want any part of the mood I'm in." Her probing may have brought on the mood, but he wouldn't let it contaminate her.

Angling down with slow precision, she pressed her lips to his. Not moving. Only their mouths and hands linked.

He wanted—needed—to move her away gently. But his fingers curled around the softness of her arm.

"Shanny," he whispered against her mouth, "tell me to leave."

"Not a chance. I only have one question."

"Go ahead." He braced himself for another emotional root canal.

She brought his hand to her chest, pressing his palm against her breast. "Do you have a condom?"

Relief splashed over him like a tidal wave. "Hell, yes, I have one, two in fact, in my wallet. Because even when we're not talking, I know the way we are together could combust at any second. And I will always, always make sure you're protected and safe."

Standing, he scooped her into his arms. Purring her approval, she hooked her hands behind his neck and tipped her face for a full kiss. The soft cushion of her breasts against his chest sent his libido into overdrive. He throbbed against the sweet curve of her hip. At the sweep of tongue, the taste of caramel and *her,* he fought the urge to follow through on the impulse to have her here, now, on the table.

He sketched his mouth along her jaw, down to her collarbone, the scent of her lavender body wash reminding him of shared showers at his place. "We need to go upstairs."

"The pantry is closer." She nipped his bottom lip. "And empty. We can lock the door. I need you now."

"Are you su—?"

"Don't even say it." She dipped her hands into the neckline of his loose shirt, her fingernails sinking insistently deep. "I want you. No waiting."

Her words closed down arguments and rational thought. He made a sure-footed beeline across the tiled floor toward the pantry. Shannon nuzzled his neck, kissed along his jaw, all the while murmuring disjointed words of need that stoked him higher—made his feet move faster. As he walked, her silky blond hair and whispery robe trailed, her sexy little heels dangling from her toes.

Dipping at the door, he flipped the handle and shouldered inside the pantry, a food storage area the size of a small bedroom. The scent of hanging dried herbs coated the air, the smell earthy. He slid her glasses from her face and set them aside on a shelf next to rows of bottled water.

As the door eased closed, the space darkened and his

other senses increased. She reached for the light switch and he clasped her wrist, stopping her.

"I don't need light to see you. Your beautiful body is fired into my memory." His fingers crawled up her leg, bunching the frothy gown along her soft thigh, farther still to just under the curve of her buttocks. "Just the feel of you is about more than my willpower can take."

"I don't want your willpower. I'm fed up with your restraint. Give me the uninhibited old Tony back." Her husky voice filled the room with unmistakable desire.

Pressing her hips closer, he tasted down her neck, charting his way to her breasts. An easy swipe cleared the fabric from her shoulders and he found a taut nipple. Damn straight he didn't need light. He knew her body, knew just how to lave and tease the taut peak until she tore at his shirt with frantic hands.

His buttons popped and cool air blanketed his back, warm Shannon writhing against his front. Hooking a finger along the rim of her bikini panties, he stroked her silky smooth stomach. Tugging lightly, he started the scrap of fabric downward until she shimmied them the rest of the way off.

Stepping closer, the silky gown bunched between them, she flattened her hand to the fly of his jeans. He went harder against the pleasure of her touch. Shannon. Just Shannon.

She unzipped his pants and freed his arousal. Clasping him in her fist, she stroked once, and again, her thumb working over his head with each glide. His eyes slammed shut.

Her other hand slipped into his back pocket and pulled out his wallet. A light crackle sounded as she tore into the packet. Her deft fingers rolled the sheath down the length of him with torturous precision.

"Now," she demanded softly against his neck. "Here. On the stepstool or against the door, I don't care as long as you're inside me."

Gnawing need chewed through the last of his restraint. She wanted this. He craved her. No more waiting. Tony backed her against the solid panel of the door, her fingernails digging into his shoulders, his back, lower as she tucked her hand inside his jeans and boxers.

Arching, urging, she hooked her leg around his, opening for him. Her shoe clattered to the floor but she didn't seem to notice or care. He nudged at her core, so damp and ready for him. He throbbed—and thrust.

Velvet heat clamped around him, drew him deeper, sent sparks shooting behind his eyelids. In the darkened room, the pure essence of Shannon went beyond anything he'd experienced. And the importance of that expanded inside him, threatening to drive him to his knees.

So he focused on her, searching with his hands and mouth, moving inside and stroking outside to make sure she was every bit as encompassed by the mind-numbing ecstasy. She rocked faster against him. Her sighs came quicker, her moans of pleasure higher and louder until he captured the sound, kissing her and thrusting with his tongue and body. He explored the soft inside of her mouth, savoring the soft clamp of her gripping him with spasms he knew signaled her approaching orgasm.

Teeth gritted, he held back his own finish. Her face pressed to his neck. Her chants of *yes, yes, yes* synced with his pulse and pounding. Still, he held back, determined to take her there once more. She bowed away from the door, into him, again and again until her teeth sunk into his shoulder on a stifled cry of pleasure.

The scent of her, of slick sex and *them* mixed with the already earthy air.

Finally—*finally*—he could let go. The wave of pleasure pulsing through him built higher, roaring louder in his ears. He'd been too long without her. The wave crested. Release crashed over him. Rippling through him. Shifting the ground under his feet until his forehead thumped against the door.

Hauling her against his chest, heart still galloping, as they both came back down to earth in the pantry.

The pantry, for God's sake?

His chances of staying away from Shannon again were slim. That path didn't work for either of them. But if they were going to be together, he would make sure their next encounter was total fantasy material.

Sun glinting along the crystal clear pool, Shannon tugged Kolby's T-shirt over his head and slid his feet into tiny Italian leather sandals. She'd spent the morning splashing with her son and Tony's sister, and she wasn't close to working off pent-up energy. Even the soothing ripple of the heated waters down the fountain rock wall hadn't stilled the jangling inside her.

After making love in the pantry, she and Tony had locked themselves in her room where he'd made intense and thorough love to her. Her skin remembered the rasp of his beard against her breasts, her stomach, the insides of her thighs. How could she still crave even more from him? She should be in search of a good nap rather than wondering when she could get Tony alone again.

Of course she would have to find him first.

He'd left via her balcony just as the morning sun peeked over the horizon. Now that big orange glow was directly overhead and no word from him. She deflated her son's water wings. The hissing air and the maternal ritual reminded her of Tony's revelations just before they'd ended up in the closet.

Could he be avoiding her to dodge talking further? He'd made no secret of using sex to skirt the painful topic. She couldn't even blame him when she'd been guilty of the same during their affair. What did this do to their deadline to return home?

Kolby yanked the hem of her cover-up. "Want another movie."

"We'll see, sweetie." Kolby was entranced by the large home theater, but then what child wouldn't be?

Tony's half sister shaded her eyes in the lounger next to them, an open paperback in her other hand. "I can take him in if you want to stay outside. Truly, I don't mind." She toyed with her silver shell necklace, straightening the conch charm.

"But you're reading. And aren't you leaving this afternoon? I don't want to keep you from your packing."

"Do you honestly think any guest of Enrique Medina is bothered by packing their own suitcases? Get real." She snorted lightly. "I have plenty of time. Besides, I've been wanting to check out the new Disney movie for my library's collection."

She'd learned Eloisa was a librarian, which explained the satchel of books she'd brought along. Her husband was an architect who specialized in restoring historic landmarks. They were an unpretentious couple caught up in a maelstrom. "What if the screening room doesn't have the movie you w—" She stopped short. "Of course they have whatever you're looking for on file."

"A bit intimidating, isn't it?" Eloisa pulled on her wraparound cover-up, tugging her silver necklace out so the conch charm was visible. "I didn't grow up with all of this and I suspect you didn't, either."

Shannon rubbed her arms, shivering in spite of the eighty-degree day. "How do you keep from letting it overwhelm you?"

"I wish I could offer you reassurance or answers, but honestly I'm still figuring out how to deal with all of this myself. I had only begun to get to know my birth father a few months ago." She looked back at the mission-style mansion, her eyebrows pinching together. "Now the whole royal angle has gone public. They haven't figured out about me. Yet. That's why we're here this week, to talk with Enrique and his attorneys, to set up some preemptive strikes."

"I'm sorry."

Thank God Eloisa had the support of her husband. And Tony had been there for her. Who was there for him? Even his brothers hadn't shown up beyond sterile conference calls.

"You have nothing to apologize for, Shannon. I'm only saying it's okay to feel overwhelmed. Cut yourself some slack and do what you can to stay level. Let me watch a movie with your son while you swim or enjoy a bubble bath or take a nap. It's okay."

Indecision warred inside her. These past couple of weeks she'd had more help with Kolby than since he was born. Guilt tweaked her maternal instincts.

"Please, Mama?" Kolby sidled closer to Eloisa. "I like Leesa."

Ah, and just like that, her maternal guilt worried in another direction, making her fret that she hadn't given her son enough play dates or socialization. Funny how a mother worried no matter what.

Shannon nodded to Tony's sister. "If you're absolutely sure."

"He's a cutie, and I'm guessing he will be asleep before

the halfway point. Enjoy the pool a while longer. It'll be good practice for me to spend time with him." She smiled whimsically as she ruffled his damp hair. "Jonah and I are hoping to have a few of our own someday."

"Thank you. I accept gratefully." Shannon remembered well what it felt like to be young and in love and hopeful for the future. She couldn't bring herself to regret Nolan since he'd given her Kolby. "I hope we'll have the chance to speak again before you leave this afternoon?"

"Don't worry." Eloisa winked. "I imagine we'll see each other again."

With a smile, Shannon hugged her little boy close, inhaling his baby fresh scent with a hint of chlorine.

He squirmed, his cheeks puffed with a wide smile. "Wanna go."

She pressed a quick kiss to his forehead. "Be good for Mrs. Landis."

Eloisa took his hand. "We'll be fine."

Kolby waved over his shoulder without a backward glance.

Too restless for a bath or nap, she eyed the pool and whipped off her cover-up. Laps sounded like the wisest option. Diving in, she stared through the chlorinated depths until her eyes burned, forcing her to squeeze them shut. She lost herself in the rhythm of slicing her arms through the heated water, no responsibilities, no outside world. Just the *thump, thump, thump* of her heart mingling with the roar of the water passing over her ears.

Five laps later, she flipped underwater and resurfaced face up for a backstroke. She opened her eyes and, oh my, the view had changed. Tony stood by the waterfall in black board shorts.

Whoa. Her stomach lurched into a swan dive. Tony's bronzed chest sprinkled with hair brought memories of their night together, senses on overload from the darkened herb-scented pantry, later in the brightly lighted luxury of her bedroom. Who would have thought dried oregano and rosemary could be aphrodisiacs?

His eyes hooked on her crocheted two piece with thorough and unmistakable admiration. He knew every inch of her body and made his appreciation clear whether she wore high-end garb or her simple black waitress uniform, wilted from a full shift. God, how he was working his way into her heart as well as her life.

She swam toward the edge with wide lazy strokes. "Is Kolby okay?"

"Enjoying the movie and popcorn." He knelt by the edge, his elbow on one knee drawing her eye to the nautical compass tattooed on his bicep. "Although with the way his head is drooping, chances are he'll be asleep anytime now."

"Thank you for checking on him." She resisted the urge to ask Tony what *he*'d been doing since he left her early this morning.

"Not a problem." His fingers played through the water in front of her without touching but so close the swirls caressed her breasts. "I said I intended to romance you and I got sidetracked. I apologize for that. The woman I'm with should be treated like a princess."

His *princess?* Shock loosened her hold on the edge of the pool. Tony caught her arm quickly and eased her from the water to sit next to him. His gaze swept her from soaking wet hair to dripping toes. Appreciation smoked, darkening his eyes to molten heat she recognized well.

He tipped her chin with a knuckle scarred from handling sailing lines. "Are you ready to be royally romanced?"

Eleven

A five-minute walk later, Tony flattened his palm to Shannon's back and guided her down the stone path leading from the mansion to the greenhouse. Her skin, warmed from the sun, heated through her thin cover-up. Soon, he hoped to see and feel every inch of her without barriers.

He'd spent the morning arranging a romantic backdrop for their next encounter. Finding privacy was easier said than done on this island, but he was persistent and creative. Anticipation ramped inside him.

He was going to make things right with her. She deserved to be treated like a princess, and he had the resources to follow through. His mind leaped ahead to all the ways he could romance her back on the mainland now that he understood her better—once he fulfilled the remaining weeks he'd promised his father.

A kink started in his neck.

Squeezing his hand lightly, she followed him along the

rocky path, the mansion smaller on the horizon. Few trees stood between them and the glass building ahead. Early on, Enrique had cleared away foliage for security purposes.

"Where are we going?"

"You'll see soon."

Farther from shore, a sprawling oak had been saved. The mammoth trunk declared it well over a hundred years old. As a kid, he'd begged to keep this one for climbing. His father had gruffly agreed. The memory kicked over him, itchy and ill timed.

He brushed aside a branch, releasing a flock of butterflies soaring toward the conservatory, complete with two wings branching off the main structure. "This is the greenhouse I told you about. It also has a café style room."

Enrique had done his damnedest to give his sons a "normal" childhood, as much as he could while never letting them off the island. Tony had undergone some serious culture shock after he'd left. At least working on a shrimper had given him time to absorb the mainland in small bites. Back then, he'd even opted to rent a sailboat for a home rather than an apartment.

As they walked past a glass gazebo, Shannon tipped her face to his. Sunlight streaked through the trees, bathing her face. "Is that why the movie room has more of a theater feel?"

Nodding, he continued, "There's a deli at the ferry station and an ice cream parlor at the creamery. I thought we could take Kolby there."

He hoped she heard his intent to try with her son as well, to give this relationship a real chance at working.

"Kolby likes strawberry flavored best," she said simply.

"I'll remember that," he assured her. And he meant it.

"We also have a small dental clinic. And of course there's the chapel."

"They've thought of everything." Her mouth oohed over a birdbath with doves drinking along the edge.

"My father always said a monarch's job was to see to the needs of his people. This island became his minikingdom. Because of the isolation, he needed to make accommodations, try to create a sense of normalcy." Clouds whispered overhead and Tony guided her faster through the garden. "He's started a new round of renovations. A number of his staff members have died of old age. That presents a new set of challenges as he replaces them with employees who aren't on the run, people who have options."

"Like Alys."

"Exactly," he said, just as the skies opened up with an afternoon shower. "Now, may I take you to lunch? I know this great little out-of-the-way place with kick-ass fresh flowers."

"Lead on." Shannon tugged up the hood on her cover-up and raced alongside him.

As the rain pelted faster, he charged up the stone steps leading to the conservatory entrance. Tony threw open the double doors, startling a sparrow into flight around the high glass ceiling in the otherwise deserted building. A quick glance around assured him that yes, everything was exactly as he'd ordered.

"Ohmigod, Tony!" Shannon gasped, taking in the floral feast for her eyes as well as her nose. "This is breathtaking."

Flipping the hood from her head, she plunged deeper into the spacious greenhouse where a riot of scents and colors waited. Classical music piped lowly from hidden speakers. Ferns dangled overhead. Unlike crowded nurseries she'd visited in the past, this space sprawled more like an indoor floral park.

An Italian marble fountain trickled below a skylight, water spilling softly from a carved snake's mouth as it curled around some reclining Roman god. Wrought iron screens sported hydrangeas and morning glories twining throughout, benches in front for reading or meditation. Potted palms and cacti added height to the interior landscape. Tiered racks of florist's buckets with cut flowers stretched along a far wall. She spun under the skylight, immersing herself in the thick perfume, sunbeams and Debussy's *Nocturnes*.

While she could understand Tony's point about not wanting to be isolated here indefinitely, she appreciated the allure of the magical retreat Enrique had created. Even the rain *tap, tap, tapping* overhead offered nature's lyrical accent to the soft music.

Slowing her spin, she found Tony staring at her with undeniable arousal. Tony, and only Tony because the space appeared otherwise deserted. Her skin prickled with awareness at the muscular display of him in nothing but board shorts and deck shoes.

"Are we alone?" she asked.

"Completely," he answered, gesturing toward a little round table set for two, with wine and finger foods. "Help yourself. There are stuffed mussels, fried squid, vegetable skewers, cold olives and cheese."

She strode past him, without touching but so close a magnetic field seemed to activate, urging her to seal her body to his.

"It's been so wonderful here indulging in grown-up food after so many meals of chicken nuggets and pizza." She broke off a corner of ripe white cheese and popped it in her mouth.

"Then you're going to love the beverage selection." Tony scooped up a bottle from the middle of the table. "Red wine from Basque country or sherry from southern Spain?"

"Red, please. But can we wait a moment on the food? I want to see everything here first."

"I was hoping you would say that." He passed her a crystal glass, half full.

She sipped, staring at him over the rim. "Perfect."

"And there's still more." His fingers linked with hers, he led her past an iron screen to a secluded corner.

Vines grew tangled and dense over the windows, the sun through the glass roof muted by rivulets of rain. A chaise longue was tucked in a corner. Flower petals speckled the furniture and floor. Everything was so perfect, so beautiful, it brought tears to her eyes. God, it still scared her how much she wanted to trust her feelings, trust the signals coming from Tony.

To hide her eyes until she could regain control, she rushed to the crystal vase of mixed flowers on the end table and buried her face in the bouquet. "What a unique blend of fragrances."

"It's a specially ordered arrangement. Each flower was selected for you because of its meaning."

Touched by the detailed thought he'd put into the encounter, she pivoted to face him. "You told me once you wanted to wrap me in flowers."

"That's the idea here." His arms banded around her waist. "And I was careful to make sure there will be no thorns. Only pleasure."

If only life could be that simple. With their time here running out, she couldn't resist.

"You're sure we won't be interrupted?" She set her wine glass on the end table and linked her fingers behind his neck. "No surveillance cameras or telephoto lenses?"

"Completely certain. There are security cameras outside, but none inside. I've given the staff the afternoon off and our guards are not Peeping Toms. We are totally and completely alone." He anchored her against him, the rigid length of his arousal pressing into her stomach with a hefty promise.

"You prepared for this." And she wanted this, wanted him. But… "I'm not sure I like being so predictable."

"You are anything but predictable. I've never met a more confusing person in my life." He tugged a damp lock of her hair. "Any more questions?"

She inhaled deeply, letting the scents fill her with courage. "Who can take off faster the other person's clothes?"

"Now there's a challenge I can't resist." He bunched her cover-up in his hands and peeled the soft cotton over her head.

Shaking her hair free, she leaned into him just as he slanted his mouth over hers. His fingers made fast work of the ties to her bathing suit top. The crocheted triangles fell away, baring her to the steamy greenhouse air.

She nipped his ear where a single dot-shaped scar stayed from a healed-over piercing. A teenage rebellion, he'd told her once. She could envision him on a Spanish galleon, a swarthy and buffed pirate king.

For a moment, for *this* moment, she let herself indulge in foolish fantasies, no fears. She would allow the experience to sweep her away as smoothly as she brushed off his board shorts. She pushed aside the sterner responsible voice inside her that insisted she remember past mistakes and tread cautiously.

"It's been too damn long." He thumbed off her swimsuit bottom.

"Uh, hello?" She kicked the last fabric barrier away and

prayed other barriers could be as easily discarded. "It's been less than eight hours since you left my room."

"Too long."

She played her fingers along the cut of his sculpted chest, down the flat plane of his washboard stomach. Pressing her lips to his shoulder, she kissed her way toward his arm until she grazed the different texture of his tattooed flesh—inked with a black nautical compass. "I've always wanted to ask why you chose this particular tattoo."

His muscles bunched and twitched. "It symbolizes being able to find my way home."

"There's still so much I don't know about you." Concerns trickled through her like the rain trying to find its way inside.

"Hey, we're here to escape. All that can wait." He slipped her glasses from her face and placed them on the end table.

Parting through the floral arrangement to the middle, he slipped out an orchid and pinched off the flower. He trailed the bloom along her nose, her cheekbones and jaw in a silky scented swirl. "For magnificence."

Her knees went wobbly and she sat on the edge of the chaise, tapestry fabric rough on the backs on her thighs, rose-petal smooth. He tucked the orchid behind her ear, easing her back until she reclined.

Returning to the vase, he tugged free a long stalk with indigo buds and explored the length of her arm, then one finger at a time. Then over her stomach to her other hand and back up again in a shivery path that left her breathless.

"Blue salvia," he said, "because I think of you night and day."

His words stirred her as much as the glide of the flower

over her shoulder. Then he placed it on the tiny pillow under her head.

A pearly calla lily chosen next, he traced her collarbone before lightly dipping between her breasts.

"Shannon," he declared hoarsely, "I chose this lily because you are a majestic beauty."

Detouring, he sketched the underside of her breast and looped round again and again, each circle smaller until he teased the dusky tip. Her body pulled tight and tingly. Her back arched into the sweet sensation and he transferred his attention to her other breast, repeating the delicious pattern.

Reaching for him, she clutched his shoulders, aching to urge him closer. "Tony…"

Gently, he clasped her wrists and tucked them at her sides. "No touching or I'll stop."

"Really?"

"Probably not, because I can't resist you." He left the lily in her open palm. "But how about you play along anyway? I guarantee you'll like the results."

Dark eyes glinting with an inner light, Tony eased free… "A coral rose for passion."

His words raspy, his face intense, he skimmed the bud across her stomach, lower. Lower still. Her head fell back, her eyes closed as she wondered just how far he would dare go.

The silky teasing continued from her hip inward, daring more and even more. A husky moan escaped between her clenched lips.

Still, he continued until the rose caressed…oh my. Her knee draped to the side giving him, giving the flower, fuller access as he teased her. Gooseflesh sprinkled her skin. Her body focused on the feelings and perfumes stoking desire higher.

A warm breath steamed over her stomach with only a second's warning before his mouth replaced the flower. Her fingers twitched into a fist, crushing the lily and releasing a fresh burst of perfume. A flick of his tongue, alternated with gentle suckles, caressed and coaxed her toward completion.

Her head thrashed as she chased her release. He took her to the brink, then retreated, drawing out the pleasure until the pressure inside her swelled and throbbed...

And bloomed.

A cry of pleasure burst free and she didn't bother holding it back. She rode the sensation, gasping in floral-tinged breaths.

His bold hands stroked upward as he slid over her, blanketing her with his hard, honed body. She hooked a languid leg over his hip. Her arm draped his shoulders as she drew him toward her, encouraging him to press inside.

The smell of crushed flowers clung to his skin as she kissed her way along his chest, back up his neck. He filled her, stretched her, moved inside her. She was surprised to feel desire rising again to a fevered pitch. Writhing, she lost herself in the barrage of sensations. The bristle of his chest hair against her breasts. The silky softness of flower petals against her back.

And the scents—she gasped in the perfect blend of musk and sex and earthy greenhouse. She raked his back, broad and strong and yet so surprisingly gentle, too.

He was working his way not only into her body but into her heart. When had she ever stood a chance at resisting him? As much as she tried to tell herself it was only physical, only an affair, she knew this man had come to mean so much more to her. He reached her in ways no one ever had before.

She grappled at the hard planes of his back, completion so close all over again.

"Let go and I'll catch you," he vowed against her ear and she believed him.

For the first time in so long, she totally trusted.

The magnitude exploded inside her, blasting through barriers. Pleasure filled every niche. Muscles knotted in Tony's back as he tensed over her and growled his own hoarse completion against her ear.

Staring up at the rain-splattered skylight, tears burning her eyes again, she held Tony close. She felt utterly bare and unable to hide any longer. She'd trusted him with her body.

Now the time had come to trust him with her secrets.

Twelve

Tony watched Shannon on his iPhone as she talked to Kolby. She'd assured him that she wanted to stay longer in their greenhouse getaway, once she checked on her son.

Raindrops pattered slowly on the skylight, the afternoon shower coming to an end. Sunshine refracted off the moisture, casting prisms throughout the indoor garden.

He had Shannon back in his bed and in his life and he intended to do anything it took to keep her there. The chemistry between them, the connection—it was one of a kind. The way she'd calmly handled his bizarre family set-up, keeping her down-to-earth ways in the face of so much wealth… Finally, he'd found a woman he could trust, a woman he could spend his life with. Coming back to the island had been a good thing after all, since it had made him realize how unaffected she was by the trappings. In a compass, she would be the magnet, a grounding center.

And he owed her so much better than he'd delivered thus

far. He'd wrecked Shannon's life. It was up to him to fix it. Here, alone with her in the bright light of day, he couldn't avoid the truth.

They would get married.

The decision settled inside him with a clean fit, so much so he wondered why he hadn't decided so resolutely before now. His feelings for her ran deep. He knew she cared for him, too. And marrying each other would solve her problems.

They were making progress. He could tell she'd been swayed by the flowers, the ambience.

A plan formed in his mind. Later tonight he would take her to the chapel, lit with candles, and he would propose, while the lovemaking they'd shared here was still fresh in her memory.

Now he just had to figure out the best way to persuade her to say yes.

Thumbing the off button, she disconnected her call. "The nanny says Kolby has only just woken up and she's feeding him a snack." She passed his phone to him and curled against his side on the chaise. "Thanks for not teasing me about being overprotective. I can't help but worry when I'm not with him."

"I would too, if he was mine," he said. Then her surprised expression prompted him to continue, "Why do you look shocked?"

"No offense meant." She smoothed a hand along his chest. "It's just obvious you and he haven't connected."

Something he would need to rectify in order to be a part of Shannon's life. "I will never let you or him down the way his father did."

She winced and he could feel her drawing back into herself. He wanted all barriers gone between them as fully as they'd tossed aside their clothes.

·

"Hey, Shannon, stay with me here." He cupped her bare hip. "I asked you before if your husband hit you and you said no. Did you lie about that?"

Sitting up abruptly, she gathered her swimsuit off the floor.

"Let's get dressed and then we can talk." She yanked on the suit bottom briskly.

Waiting, he slid on his board shorts. She tied the bikini strings behind her neck with exaggerated effort, all the while staring at the floor. A curtain of tousled blond locks covered her face. Just when he'd begun to give up on getting an answer, she straightened, shaking her hair back over her shoulders.

"I was telling the truth when I said Nolan never laid a hand on me. But there are things I need to explain in order for you to understand why it's so difficult for me to accept help." Determination creased her face. "Nolan was always a driven man. His perfectionism made him successful in business. And I'd been brought up to believe marriage is forever. How could I leave a man because he didn't like the way I hung clothes in the closet?"

He forced his hands to stay loose on his knees, keeping his body language as unthreatening as possible when he already sensed he would want to beat the hell out of Nolan Crawford by the end of this conversation—if he wasn't already dead.

Plucking a flower petal from her hair, she rubbed the coral-colored patch between two fingers. "Do you know how many people laughed at me because I was upset that he didn't want me to work? He said he wanted us to have more time together. Somehow any plans I made with others were disrupted. After a while I lost contact with my friends."

The picture of isolation came together in his head with startling clarity. He understood the claustrophobic feeling of being cut off from the rest of the world. Although he couldn't help but think his father's need to protect his children differed from an obsessive—abusive—husband dominating his wife. Rage simmered, ready to boil.

She scooped her cover-up from the floor and clutched it to her stomach. "Then I got pregnant. Splitting up became more complicated."

Hating like hell the helpless feeling, he passed her glasses back to her. It was damn little, but all he could see her accepting from him right now.

With a wobbly smile, she slid them on her face and seemed to take strength from them. "When Kolby was about thirteen months old, he spiked a scary high fever while I was alone with him. Nolan had always gone with us to pediatric check-ups. At the ER, I was a mess trying to give the insurance information. I had no idea what to tell them, because Nolan had insisted I not 'worry' about such things as medical finances. That day triggered something in me. I needed to take care of my son."

He took her too-cold hand and rubbed it between his.

"Looking back now I see the signs were there. Nolan's computer and cell phone were password protected. He considered it an invasion of privacy if I asked who he was speaking to. I thought he was cheating. I never considered…"

He squeezed her hand in silent encouragement.

"So I decided to learn more about the finances, because if I needed to leave him, I had to make sure my son's future was protected and not spirited away to some Cayman account." She fidgeted, her fingers landing on the blue salvia—*I think of you often* took on a darker meaning. "I was lucky enough to figure out his computer password."

"*You* discovered the Ponzi scheme?" Good God,

what kind of strength would it take to turn in her own husband?

"It was the hardest thing I've ever done, but I handed over the evidence to the police. He'd stolen so much from so many people, I couldn't stay silent. His parents posted bail, and I wasn't given warning." She spun the stem between her thumb and forefinger. "When he walked back into the house, he had a gun."

Shock nailed him harder than a sail boom to the gut.

"My God, Shannon. I knew he'd committed suicide but I had no idea you were there. I'm so damn sorry."

"That's not all, though. For once the media didn't uncover everything." She drew herself up straight. "Nolan said he was going to kill me, then Kolby and then himself."

Her words iced the perspiration on his brow. This was so much worse than he'd foreseen. He cupped an arm around her shoulders and pulled her close. She trembled and kept twirling the flower, but she didn't stop speaking.

"His parents pulled up in the driveway." A shuddering sigh racked her body, her profile pained. "He realized he wouldn't have time to carry out his original plan. Thank God he locked himself in his office before he pulled the trigger and killed himself."

"Shannon." Horror threatened to steal his breath, but for her, he would hold steady. "I don't even know what to say to fix the hell you were put through."

"I didn't tell his parents what he'd planned. They'd lost their son and he'd been labeled a criminal." She held up the blue salvia. "I couldn't see causing them more grief when they thought of him."

Her eyes were filled with tears and regret. Tony kissed her forehead, then pulled her against his chest. "You were generous to the memory of a man who didn't deserve it."

"I didn't do it for him. No matter what, he's the father

of my child." She pressed her cheek harder against him and hugged him tightly. "Kolby will have to live with the knowledge that his dad was a crook, but I'll be damned before I'll let my son know his own father tried to kill him."

"You've fought hard for your son." He stroked her back. "You're a good mother and a strong woman."

She reminded him of a distant memory, of his own mother wrapping him in a silver blanket as they left San Rinaldo and telling him the shield would keep him safe. She'd been right. If only he could have protected her, as well.

Easing away, Shannon scrubbed her damp cheeks. "Thank God for Vernon. I'd sold off everything to pay Nolan's debts, even my piano and my oboe. The first waitressing job I landed in Louisiana didn't cover expenses. We were running out of options when Vernon hired me. Everyone else treated me like a pariah. Even Nolan's parents didn't want anything to do with either of us. So many people insisted I must have known what he was doing. That I must have tucked away money for myself. The gossip and the rumors were hell."

Realization, understanding spewed inside him like the abrupt shower of the sprinklers misting over the potted plants. He'd finally found a woman he could trust enough to propose marriage.

Only to find a husband was likely the last thing she ever wanted again.

Three hours later, Shannon sat on the floor in her suite with Kolby, rolling wooden trains along a ridged track. An ocean breeze spiraled through the open balcony door. She craved the peace of that boundless horizon. Never again would she allow herself to be hedged in as she'd been in her marriage.

After she'd finished dredging up her past, she'd needed to see her son. Tony had been understanding, although she could sense he wanted to talk longer. Once she'd returned to her suite, she'd showered and changed—and had been with her son ever since.

The past twenty-four hours had been emotionally charged on so many levels. Tony had been supportive and understanding, while giving her space. He'd also been a tender—thorough—lover.

Could she risk giving their relationship another try once they returned to the mainland? Was it possible for her to be a part of a normal couple?

A tug on her shirt yanked her attention back to the moment. Kolby looked up at her with wide blue eyes. "I'm hungry."

"Of course, sweetie. We'll go down to the kitchen and see what we can find." Hopefully the cook—the *chef*— wouldn't object since he must be right in the middle of supper prep. "We just need to clean up the toys first."

As she reached for the train set's storage bin, she heard a throat clear behind her and jerked around to find her on-again lover standing in the balcony doorway.

Her stomach fluttered with awareness, and she pressed her sweaty palms to her jeans. "How long have you been there?"

"Not long." Tony had showered and changed as well, wearing khakis and a button-down. "I can make his snack."

Whoa, Tony was seeking time with her son? That signaled a definite shift in their relationship. Although she'd seen him make his own breakfast in the past, she couldn't miss the significance of this moment and his efforts to try.

Turning him away would mean taking a step back. "Are you sure?"

Because God knows, she still had a boatload of fears.

"Positive," he said, his voice as steady as the man.

"Okay then." She pressed a hand over her stomach full of butterflies. "I'll just clean up here—"

"We've got it, don't we, pal?"

Kolby eyed him warily but he didn't turn away, probably because Tony kept his distance. He wasn't pushing. Maybe they'd both learned a lot these past couple of weeks.

"Okay, then." She stood, looking around the room, unsure what to do next. "I'll just, uh…"

Tony touched her hand lightly. "You mentioned selling your piano and I couldn't miss the regret in your voice. There's a Steinway Grand in the east wing. Alys or one of the guards can show you where if you would like to play."

Would she? Her fingers twitched. She'd closed off so much of her old life, including the good parts. Her music had been a beautiful bright spot in those solitary years of her life with Nolan. How kind of Tony to see beyond the surface of the harrowing final moments that had tainted her whole marriage. In the same way he'd chosen flowers based on facets of her personality, he'd detected the creativity she'd all but forgotten, honoring it in a small, simple offer.

Nodding her head was tougher than she thought. Her body went a little jerky before she could manage a response. "I would like that. Thank you for thinking of it and for spending time with Kolby."

He was a man who saw beyond her material needs…a man to treasure.

Her throat clogging with emotion, she backed from the room, watching the tableau of Tony with her son. Antonio Medina, a prince and billionaire, knelt on the floor with Kolby, cleaning up a wooden train set.

Tony chunked the caboose in the bin. "Has your mom ever cooked you a Cyclops?"

"What's a cycle-ops?" His face was intent with interest.

"The sooner we clean up the trains, the sooner I can show you."

She pressed a hand to her swelling heart. Tony was handling Kolby with ease. Her son would be fine.

After getting directions from Alys, Shannon found the east wing and finally the music room. What a simple way to describe such an awe-inspiring space. More of a circular ballroom, wooden floors stretched across, with a coffered ceiling that added texture as well as sound control. Crystal chandeliers and sconces glittered in the late afternoon sun.

And the instruments… Her feet drew her deeper into the room, closer to the gold gilded harp and a Steinway grand piano. She stroked the ivory keys reverently, then zipped through a scale. Pure magic.

She perched on the bench, her hands poised. Unease skittered up her spine like a double-timed scale, a sense of being watched. Pivoting around, she searched the expansive room….

Seated in a tapestry wingback, Enrique Medina stared back at her from beside a stained glass window. Even with his ill health, the deposed monarch radiated power and charisma. His dogs asleep on either side, he wore a simple dark suit with an ascot, perfectly creased although loose fitting. He'd lost even more weight since her arrival.

Enrique thumbed a gold pocket watch absently. "Do not mind me."

Had Tony sent her to this room on purpose, knowing his father would be here? She didn't think so, given the stilted relationship between the two men. "I don't want to disturb you."

"Not at all. We have not had a chance to speak alone, you and I," he said with a hint of an accent.

The musicality was pleasing to the ear. Every now and then, a lilt in certain words reminded her of how Tony spoke, small habits that she hadn't discerned as being raised with a foreign language. But she could hear the similarity more clearly when listening to his father.

While she'd seen the king daily during her two weeks on the island, those encounters had been mostly during meals. He'd spent the majority of his time with his daughter. But since Eloisa and her husband had left this afternoon, Enrique must be at loose ends. Shannon envied them that connection, and missed her own parents all the more. How much different her life might have been if they hadn't died. Her mother had shared a love of music.

She stroked the keyboard longingly. "Who plays the piano?"

"My sons took lessons as a part of the curriculum outlined by their tutors."

"Of course, I should have realized," she said. "Tony can play?"

Laughter rattled around inside his chest. "That would be a stretch. My youngest son can read music, but he did not enjoy sitting still. Antonio rushed through lessons so he could go outside."

"I can picture that."

"You know him well then." His sharp brown eyes took in everything. "Now my middle boy, Duarte, is more disciplined, quite the martial arts expert. But with music?" Enrique waved dismissively. "He performs like a robot."

Her curiosity tweaked for more details on Tony's family. Over the past couple of weeks, their relationship had deepened, and she needed more insights to still the fears churning her gut. "And your oldest son, Carlos? How did he fare with the piano lessons?"

A dark shadow crossed Enrique's face before he schooled his regal features again. "He had a gift. He's a surgeon now, using that touch in other ways."

"I can see how the two careers could tap into the same skill," she said, brushing her fingers over the gleaming keys.

Perhaps she could try again to find a career that tapped into her love of music. What a gift it would be to bring joy deeper into her life again.

Enrique tucked one hand into his pocket. "Do you have feelings for my son?"

His blunt question blindsided her, but she should have realized this cunning man never chatted just for conversation's sake. "That is a personal question."

"And I may not have time to wait around for you to feel comfortable answering."

"You're playing the death card? That's a bit cold, don't you think, sir?"

He laughed, hard and full-out like Tony did—or like he used to. "You have a spine. Good. You are a fine match for my stubborn youngest."

Her irritation over his probing questions eased. What parent didn't want to see their children settled and happy? "I appreciate your opening your home to me and my son and giving us a chance to get to know you."

"Diplomatically said, my dear. You are wise to proceed thoughtfully. Regrets are a terrible thing," he said somberly. "I should have sent my family out of San Rinaldo sooner. I waited too long and Beatriz paid the price."

The darker turn of the conversation stilled her. She'd wanted more insights into Tony's life, yet this was going so much deeper than she had anticipated.

Enrique continued, "It was such chaos that day when the coup began. We had planned for my family to take one escape route and I would use another." His jaw flexed sharply in his gaunt face. "I made it out, and the rebels found my family. Carlos was injured trying to save his mother."

The picture of violence and terror he painted sounded like something from a movie, so unreal, yet they'd lived it. "Tony and your other sons witnessed the attack on their mother?"

"Antonio had nightmares for a year, and then he became obsessed with the beach and surfing. From that day on, he lived to leave the island."

She'd known the bare bones details of their escape. But the horror they'd lived through, the massive losses rolled over her with a new vividness. Tony's need to help her had more to do with caring than control. He didn't want to isolate her or smother her by managing everything the way her husband had. Tony tried to help her because he'd failed to save someone else he cared about.

Somehow, knowing this made it easier for her to open her heart. To take a chance beyond their weeks here.

Without question, he would have to understand her need for independence, but she also had to appreciate how he'd been hurt, how those hurts had shaped him. And as Antonio Medina and Tony Castillo merged in her mind, she couldn't ignore the truth any longer.

She loved him.

Approaching footsteps startled her, drawing her focus from the past and toward the arched entry. Tony stepped into view just when her defenses were at their lowest. No doubt her heart was in her eyes. She started toward him, only to realize *his* eyes held no tender feelings.

The harsh angles of his face blared a forewarning before he announced, "There's been a security breach."

Thirteen

Shock jolted through Shannon, followed closely by fear. "A security breach? Where's Kolby?"

She shot to her feet and ran across the music room to Tony. The ailing king reached for his cane, his dogs waking instantly, beating her there by a footstep. Enrique steadied himself with a hand against the wall, but he was up and moving. "What happened?"

"Kolby is fine. No one has been hurt, but we have taken another hit in the media."

Enrique asked, "Have they located the island?"

"No," Tony said as Alys slid into view behind him. "It happened at the airport when Eloisa and Jonah's flight landed in South Carolina. The press was waiting, along with crowds of everyday people wanting a picture to sell for an easy buck."

Shannon's stomach lurched at another assault in the

news. "Could the frenzy have to do with the Landis family connections?"

"No," Tony said curtly. "The questions were all about their vacation with Eloisa's father the king."

Alys angled past Tony with a wheelchair. "Your Majesty, I'll take you to your office so you can speak to security directly."

The king dropped into the wheelchair heavily. "Thank you, Alys." His dogs loped into place alongside him. "I am ready."

Nerves jangled, Shannon started to follow, but Tony extended a hand to stop her.

"We need to talk."

His chilly voice stilled her feet faster than any arm across the entranceway. Had he been holding back because of concerns for his father's health? "What's wrong? What haven't you told me?"

She stepped closer for comfort. He crossed his arms over his chest.

"The leak came from this house. There was a call placed from here this afternoon—at just the right time—to an unlisted cell number."

"Here? But your father's security has been top notch." No wonder he was so concerned.

Tony unclipped his iPhone from his waistband. "We have security footage of the call being made."

Thumbing the controls, he filled the screen with a still image of a woman on the phone, a woman in a white swimsuit cover-up, hood pulled over her head.

A cover-up just like hers? "I don't understand. You think this is *me?* Why would I tip off the media?"

His mouth stayed tight-lipped and closed, and his eyes... Oh God, she recognized well that condemning look from the days following Nolan's arrest and then his death.

Steady. Steady. She reminded herself Tony wasn't Nolan or the other people who'd betrayed her, and he had good reasons to be wary. She drew in a shuddering breath.

"I understand that Enrique brought you up to be unusually cautious about the people in your life. And he had cause after what happened to your mother." Thoughts of Tony as a small child watching his mother's murder brushed sympathy over her own hurt. "But you have to see there's nothing about me that would hint at this kind of behavior."

"I know you would do anything to secure your son's future. Whoever sold this information received a hefty pay-off." He stared back at her with cold eyes and unswerving surety.

In a sense he was right. She would do anything for Kolby. But again, Tony had made a mistake. He'd offered her money before, assuming that would equate security to her. She had deeper values she wanted to relay to her son, like the importance of earning a living honorably. Tony had needed to prove that himself in leaving the island. Why was it so difficult to understand she felt the same way?

Her sympathy for him could only stretch so far.

"You actually believe I betrayed you? That I placed everyone here at risk for a few dollars?" Anger frothed higher and higher inside her. "I never wanted any of this. My son and I can get by just fine without you and your movie theater." She swatted his arm. "Answer me, damn you."

"I don't know what to think." He pinched the bridge of his nose. "Tell me it was an accident. You called a friend just to shoot the breeze because you were homesick and that friend sold you out."

Except as she'd already told him and he must remember, she didn't have friends, not anymore. Apparently she didn't even have Tony. "I'm not going to defend myself to you. Either you trust me or you don't."

He gripped her shoulders, his touch careful, his eyes more tumultuous. "I want a future with you. God, Shannon, I was going to ask you to marry me later tonight. I planned to take you back to the chapel, go inside this time and propose."

Her heart squeezed tight at the image he painted. If this security nightmare hadn't occurred, she would have been swept off her feet. She would have been celebrating her engagement with him tonight, because by God, she would have said yes. Now, that wasn't possible.

"You honestly thought we could get married when you have so little faith in me?" The betrayal burned deep. And hadn't she sworn she'd never again put herself in a position to feel that sting from someone she cared about? "You should have included some azaleas in the bouquet you chose for us. I hear they mean fragile passion."

She shrugged free of his too tempting touch. The hole inside her widened, ached.

"Damn it all, Shannon, we're talking." He started toward her.

"Stop." She held up a hand. "Don't come near me. Not now. Not ever."

"Where are you going?" He kept his distance this time. "I need to know you're safe."

"Has the new security system been installed at my apartment?"

His mouth tight, he nodded. "But we're still working on the restraining orders. Given the renewed frenzy because of Eloisa's identity—"

"The new locks and alarms will do for now."

"Damn it, Shannon—"

"I have to find Alys so she can make the arrangements."

She held her chin high. Pride and her child were all she had left now that her heart was shattered to pieces. "Kolby and I are returning to Texas."

"Where are Shannon and her son?"

His father's question hammered Tony's already pounding head. In his father's study, he poured himself three fingers of cognac, bypassing the Basque wine and the memories it evoked. Shannon wrapped around him, the scent of lilies in her hair. "You know full well where she is. Nothing slips past you here."

They'd spent the past two hours assessing the repercussions of the leak. The media feeding frenzy had been rekindled with fresh fuel about Eloisa's connection to the family. Inevitable, yet still frustrating. It gnawed at his gut to think Shannon had something to do with this, although he reassured himself it must have been an accident.

And if she'd simply slipped up and made a mistake, he could forgive her. She hadn't lived the Medina way since the cradle. Remembering all the intricacies involved in maintaining such a high level of security was difficult. If she would just admit what happened, they could move on.

His father rolled back from the computer desk, his large dogs tracking his every move from in front of the fireplace. "Apparently I do not know everything happening under my roof, because somebody placed a call putting Eloisa's flight at risk. I trusted someone I shouldn't have."

"You trusted me and my judgment." He scratched his tightening rib cage.

His father snorted with impatience. "Do not be an impulsive jackass. Think with your brain and not your heart."

"Like you've always done?" Tony snapped, his patience for his father's cryptic games growing short. "No thank you."

Once he finished his one-month obligation, he wouldn't set foot on this godforsaken island again. If memories of his life here before were unhappy, now they were gut-wrenching. His father should come to the mainland anyway for medical treatment. Even Enrique's deep coffers couldn't outfit the island with unlimited hospital options.

Enrique poured himself a drink and downed it swiftly. "I let my heart guide me when I left San Rinaldo. I was so terrified something would happen to my wife and sons that I did not think through our escape plan properly."

Invincible Enrique was admitting a mistake? Tony let that settle inside him for a second before speaking.

"You set yourself up as a diversion. Sounds pretty self-less to me." He'd never doubted his father's bravery or cool head.

"I did not think it through." He refilled his glass and stared into the amber liquid, signs of regret etched deep in his forehead. Illness had never made the king appear weak, but at this moment, the ghosts of an old past showed a vulnerability Tony had never seen before. "If I had, I would have taken into account the way Carlos would react if things went to hell. I arrogantly considered my plan foolproof. Again, I thought with my emotions and those assassins knew exactly how to target my weakness."

Tony set aside his glass without touching a drop. Empathy for his father seared him more fully than alcohol. Understanding how it felt to have his feelings ripped up through his throat because of a woman gave him insights to his father he'd never expected. "You did your best at the time."

Could he say the same when it came to Shannon?

"I tried to make that right with this island. I did every-thing in my power to create a safe haven for my sons."

"But we all three left the protection of this place."

"That doesn't matter to me. My only goal was keeping you safe until adulthood. By the time you departed, you took with you the skills to protect yourself, to make your way in the world. That never would have been possible if you'd grown up with obligations to a kingdom. For that, I'm proud."

Enrique's simply spoken words enveloped him. Even though his father wasn't telling him anything he didn't already know, something different took root in him. An understanding. Just as his mother had made the silver security blanket as a "shield," to make him feel protected, his father had been doing the same. His methods may not have been perfect, but their situation had been far from normal. They'd all been scrambling to patch together their lives.

Some of his understanding must have shown on his face, because his father smiled approvingly.

"Now, son, think about Shannon logically rather than acting like a love-sick boy."

Love-sick boy? Now that stung more than a little. And the reason? Because it was true. He did love her, and that had clouded his thinking.

He loved her. And he'd let his gut drive his conclusions rather than logic. He forced his slugging heart to slow and collected what he knew about Shannon. "She's a naturally cautious woman who wouldn't do anything to place her son at risk. If she had a call to make, she would check with you or I to make sure the call was safe. She wouldn't have relied on anyone else's word when it comes to Kolby."

"What conclusion does that lead you to?"

"We never saw the caller's face. I made an assumption

based on a female in a bathing suit cover-up. The caller must have been someone with detailed knowledge of our security systems in order to keep her face shielded. A woman of similar build. A person with something to gain and little loyalty to the Medinas…" His brain settled on… "Alys?"

"I would bet money on it." The thunderous anger Enrique now revealed didn't bode well for the assistant who'd used her family connections to take advantage of an ailing king with an aging staff. "She was even the one to order Shannon's clothes. It would be easy to make sure she had the right garb…."

Shannon had done nothing wrong.

"God, I wonder if Alys could have even been responsible for tipping off the Global Intruder about that photo of Duarte when it first ran, before he was identified." The magnitude of how badly he'd screwed up threatened to kick his knees out from under him. He braced a hand on his father's shoulder, touching his dad for the first time in fourteen years. "Where the hell is Alys?"

Enrique swallowed hard. He clapped his hand over Tony's for a charged second before clearing his throat.

"Leave Alys to me." His royal roots showed through again as he assumed command. "Don't you have a more pressing engagement?"

Tony checked his watch. He had five minutes until the ferry pulled away for the airstrip. No doubt his father would secure the proof of Alys's deception soon, but Shannon needed—hell, she deserved—to know that he'd trusted in her innocence without evidence.

He had a narrow, five-minute window to prove just how much he loved and trusted her.

* * *

The ferry horn wailed, signaling they were disconnecting from the dock. The crew was stationed at their posts, lost in the ritual of work.

Kolby on her hip, Shannon looked at the exotic island for the last time. This was hard, so much harder than she'd expected. How would she ever survive going back to Galveston where even more memories of Tony waited? She couldn't. She would have to start over somewhere new and totally different.

Except there was no place she could run now that would be free of Medina reminders. The grocery store aisles would sport gossip rags. Channel surfing could prove hazardous. And she didn't even want to think of how often she would be confronted with Tony's face peering back at her from an internet headline, reminding her of how little faith he'd had in her. As much as she wanted to say to hell with it all and accept whatever he offered, she wouldn't settle for half measures ever again.

Tears blurred the exotic shoreline, sea oats dotting the last bit of sand as they pulled away. She squeezed her eyes closed, tears cool on her heated cheeks.

"Mommy?" Kolby patted her face.

She scavenged a wobbly smile and focused on his precious face. "I'm okay, sweetie. Everything's going to be fine. Let's look for a dolphin."

"Nu-uh," he said. "Why's Tony running? Can he come wif us, pretty pwease?"

What? She followed the path of her son's pointing finger....

Tony sprinted down the dock, his mouth moving but his words swallowed up by the roar of the engines and churning water behind the ferry. Her heart pumped in time with his long-legged strides. She almost didn't dare hope, but then Tony had always delivered the unexpected.

Lowering Kolby to the deck with one arm, she leaned over the rail, straining to hear what he said. Still, the wind whipped his words as the ferry inched away. Disappointment pinched as she realized she would have to wait for the ferry to travel back again to speak to him. So silly to be impatient, but her heart had broken a lifetime's worth in one day.

Just as she'd resigned herself to waiting, Tony didn't stop running. Oh my God, he couldn't actually be planning to—

Jump.

Her heart lodged in her throat for an expanded second as he was airborne. Then he landed on deck with the surefooted ease of an experienced boater. Tony strode toward her with even, determined steps, the crew parting to make way.

He extended his hand, his fist closed around a clump of sea oats, still dripping from where he'd yanked them up. "You'll have to use your imagination here because I didn't have much time." He passed her one stalk. "Imagine this is a purple hyacinth, the 'forgive me' flower. I hope you will accept it, along with my apology."

"Go ahead. I'm listening." Although she didn't take his pretend hyacinth. He had a bit more talking to do after what he'd put her through.

Kolby patted his leg for attention. Winking down at the boy, Tony passed him one of the sea oats, which her son promptly waved like a flag. With Kolby settled, Tony shifted his attention back to Shannon.

"I've been an idiot," he said. Sea spray dampened his hair, increasing the rebellious curls. "I should have known you wouldn't do anything to put Kolby or my family at risk.

And if you'd done so inadvertently, you would have been upfront about it." He told her all the things she'd hoped to hear earlier.

While she appreciated the romanticism of his gesture, a part of her still ached that he'd needed proof. Trust was such a fragile thing, but crucial in any relationship.

"What brought about this sudden insight to my character? Did you find some new surveillance tape that proves my innocence?"

"I spoke to my father. He challenged me, made me think with my head instead of my scared-as-hell heart. And thank God he did, because once I looked deeper I realized Alys must have made the call. I can't help but wonder if she's the one who made the initial leak to the press. We don't have proof yet, but we'll find it."

Alys? Shannon mulled over that possibility, remembering the way the assistant had stared at Tony with such hunger. She'd sensed the woman wanted to be a Medina. Perhaps Alys had also wanted all the public princess perks to go with it rather than a life spent in hiding.

Tony extended his hand with the sea oats again, tickling them across Kolby's chin lightly before locking eyes with Shannon. "But none of that matters if you don't trust me."

Touching the cottony white tops of the sea oats, she weighed her words carefully. This moment could define the rest of her life. "I realize the way you've grown up has left marks on you…what happened with your mother… living in seclusion here. But I can't always worry when that's going to make you push me away again just because you're afraid I'll betray you."

Her fingers closed around his. "I've had so many people turn away from me. I can't—I won't—spend my life proving myself to you."

"And I don't expect you to." He clasped both hands around hers, his skin callused and tough, a little rough around the edges like her impetuous lover. "You're absolutely right. I was wrong. What I feel for you, it's scary stuff. But the thought of losing you is a helluva lot scarier than any alternative."

"What exactly are you saying?" She needed him to spell it out, every word, every promise.

"My life is complicated and comes with a lot more cons than pros. There's nothing to stop Alys from spilling everything she knows, and if so, it's really going to hit the fan. A life with me won't be easy. To the world, I am a Medina. And I hope you will consent to be a Medina, too."

He knelt in front of her with those sea oats—officially now her favorite plant.

"Shannon, will you be my bride? Let me be your husband and a father to Kolby." He paused to ruffle the boy's hair, eliciting a giant smile from her son. "As well as any other children we may have together. I can't promise I won't be a jackass again. I can almost guarantee that I will. But I vow to stick with it, stick with us, because you mean too much to me for me to ever mess this up again."

Sinking to her knees, she fell into his arms, her son enclosed in the circle. "Yes, I'll marry you and build a family and future with you. Tony Castillo, Antonio Medina, and any other name you go by, I love you, too. You've stolen my heart for life."

"Thank God." He gathered her closer, his arms trembling just a hint.

She lost track of how long they knelt that way until Kolby squirmed between them, and she heard the crew applauding and cheering. Together, she and Tony stood as the ferry captain shouted orders to turn the boat around.

Standing at the deck with Tony, she stared at the approaching island, a place she knew they would visit over the years. She clasped his arm, her cheek against his compass tattoo. Tony rested his chin on her head.

His breath caressed her hair. "The legend about the compass is true. I've found my way home."

Surprised, she glanced up at him. "Back to the island?"

Shaking his head, he tucked a knuckle under her chin and brushed a kiss across her mouth. "Ah, Shanny, *you* are my home."

* * * * *

COMING NEXT MONTH

Available December 7, 2010

#2053 THE TYCOON'S PATERNITY AGENDA
Michelle Celmer
Man of the Month

#2054 WILL OF STEEL
Diana Palmer
The Men of Medicine Ridge

#2055 INHERITING HIS SECRET CHRISTMAS BABY
Heidi Betts
Dynasties: The Jarrods

#2056 UNDER THE MILLIONAIRE'S MISTLETOE
"The Wrong Brother"—Maureen Child
"Mistletoe Magic"—Sandra Hyatt

#2057 DANTE'S MARRIAGE PACT
Day Leclaire
The Dante Legacy

#2058 SWEET SURRENDER, BABY SURPRISE
Kate Carlisle

REQUEST YOUR FREE BOOKS!

2 FREE NOVELS
PLUS 2
FREE GIFTS!

Passionate, Powerful, Provocative!

HARLEQUIN®

A *Romance*

FOR EVERY MOOD™

Spotlight on
Classic

Quintessential, modern love stories
that are romance at its finest.

See the next page
to enjoy a sneak peek from
the Harlequin® Romance series.

*See below for a sneak peek from our classic
Harlequin® Romance® line.*

Introducing DADDY BY CHRISTMAS by Patricia Thayer.

MIA caught sight of Jarrett when he walked into the open lobby. It was hard not to notice the man. In a charcoal business suit with a crisp white shirt and striped tie covered by a dark trench coat, he looked more Wall Street than small-town Colorado.

Mia couldn't blame him for keeping his distance. He was probably tired of taking care of her.

Besides, why would a man like Jarrett McKane be interested in her? Why would he want to take on a woman expecting a baby? Yet he'd done so many things for her. He'd been there when she'd needed him most. How could she not care about a man like that?

Heart pounding in her ears, she walked up behind him. Jarrett turned to face her. "Did you get enough sleep last night?"

"Yes, thanks to you," she said, wondering if he'd thought about their kiss. Her gaze went to his mouth, then she quickly glanced away. "And thank you for not bringing up my meltdown."

Jarrett couldn't stop looking at Mia. Blue was definitely her color, bringing out the richness of her eyes.

"What meltdown?" he said, trying hard to focus on what she was saying. "You were just exhausted from lack of sleep and worried about your baby."

He couldn't help remembering how, during the night, he'd kept going in to watch her sleep. How strange was that? "I hope you got enough rest."

She nodded. "Plenty. And you're a good neighbor for

coming to my rescue."

He tensed. Neighbor? *What neighbor kisses you like I did?* "That's me, just the full-service landlord," he said, trying to keep the sarcasm out of his voice. He started to leave, but she put her hand on his arm.

"Jarrett, what I meant was you went beyond helping me." Her eyes searched his face. "I've asked far too much of you."

"Did you hear me complain?"

She shook her head. "You should. I feel like I've taken advantage."

"Like I said, I haven't minded."

"And I'm grateful for everything…"

Grasping her hand on his arm, Jarrett leaned forward. The memory of last night's kiss had him aching for another. "I didn't do it for your gratitude, Mia."

Gorgeous tycoon Jarrett McKane has never believed in Christmas—but he can't help being drawn to soon-to-be-mom Mia Saunders! Christmases past were spent alone…and now Jarrett may just have a fairy-tale ending for all his Christmases future!

Available December 2010,
only from Harlequin® Romance®.

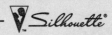

SILHOUETTE

SPECIAL EDITION

USA TODAY BESTSELLING AUTHOR

MARIE FERRARELLA

BRINGS YOU ANOTHER
HEARTWARMING STORY FROM

When Lilli McCall disappeared on him
after he proposed, Kullen Manetti swore
never to fall in love again. Eight years later
Lilli is back in his life, threatening to break
down all the walls he's put up to
safeguard his heart.

UNWRAPPING
THE PLAYBOY

Available December
wherever books are sold.

Bestselling Harlequin Presents® author

Julia James

brings you her most powerful book yet…

FORBIDDEN OR
FOR BEDDING?

The shamed mistress…

Guy de Rochemont's name is a byword for wealth
and power—and now his duty is to wed.

Alexa Harcourt knows she can never be anything
more than *The de Rochemont Mistress*.

But Alexa—the one woman Guy wants—is also
the one woman whose reputation
forbids him to take her as his wife….

**Available from Harlequin Presents
December 2010**